D1561416

The Fiery Vixen

Fate of the Worthingtons

Laura A. Barnes

Copyright © 2022 by Laura A. Barnes

All rights reserved.

No portion of this book may be reproduced in any form without written permission from the publisher or author, except as permitted by U.S. copyright law.

This is a work of fiction. Names, characters, places, and incidents either are products of the author's imagination or are used fictitiously. Any resemblance to actual events or locales or persons, living or dead, is entirely coincidental.

First Printing: 2022

Laura A. Barnes

www.lauraabarnes.com

Cover Art by Laura A. Barnes

Editor: Telltail Editing

To Will – Thank you for your patience & support

The Fiery Vixen

Prologue

A few years ago

"YOU UNDERSTAND THAT IF I assist you in this matter, you will, in return, assist me with whatever task I assign to you," Colebourne stated.

Victor Falcone understood the Duke of Colebourne's requirement if he accepted the offer. And it was one he must accept because he had no one else to rely on. If his family discovered the mess he had involved himself in, they would insist on helping him. That would tarnish their family name with a scandal they could never recover from.

His sister had already suffered from an arranged marriage with a groom who ignored her to the point where she sought companionship elsewhere. Rumors circulated of her affair. Falcone refused to cause more shame upon his family. He must face the consequences done by his own hand.

"I am aware of what is required of me if you make my sins disappear." Falcone sat up straight in the chair.

Colebourne took a drag of his cigar, his gaze scrutinizing the marquess. "Consider your sins gone. However, you also must promise to never return to the vices that brought you to this point."

"I have learned my lesson," Falcone gritted between his teeth.

His frustration lay within himself for sinking so low. However, the duke reprimanding him like a small child brought forth his irritation. A price he must pay for absolution.

Colebourne tapped his ashes into the cigar tray before stubbing it out. "We shall see. You may leave. Our business has concluded."

Falcone's eyebrows drew together in confusion. "What is it you require of me?"

"Nothing for the moment."

"But . . ."

Colebourne shuffled the papers on his desk, looking for a particular letter. "I shall contact you when I need your assistance."

Falcone's lips curled into a snarl. The duke's dismissal of him as if he were an unimportant nuisance fueled his irritation. He had hoped to earn off his favor immediately, but it would appear Colebourne had other plans for him. He stalked toward the door.

However, Colebourne threw out one more condition to his deal before he left. "Also, one last detail concerning our agreement. You will suffer through your silence if I require you to do so. Understand?"

Falcone's hand tightened on the doorknob. He debated for a brief second to call off the arrangement, but in the end, he submitted to the duke's demands. With a nod that he understood, Falcone strode from the duke's study.

He heard the lighthearted laughter of the duke's wards drifting through the house and envied their innocence. A past he longed to return to. Instead, he must continue to live in a jaded existence brought about by a life of sin he had once taken pleasure in.

Colebourne watched the young lord storm out of his study. He sat back in his chair, drumming his fingers against the desk as he thought over his decision to help Falcone out of his troubles. Falcone differed from the other souls he helped. They held remorse for the predicaments they landed in, while Falcone only held bitterness from walking away from the degenerate lifestyle he had led. Also, the boy's temper needed to be brought under control.

He hoped he didn't make a mistake with their agreement. Falcone had the skills for the tasks Colebourne would require of him. But would he gain the gentleman's loyalty or would Falcone betray him if he forced his hand?

Only time would tell.

Chapter One

THE LONGER VICTOR FALCONE waited for the Duke of Colebourne to acknowledge him, the more his irritation suffocated him. He had waited for over an hour for the duke to declare the reason for his summons. Falcone didn't have to guess why the duke requested an audience. He held information that would destroy one family's standing in society. Not just any family, but the family his niece Evelyn had married into. The Worthingtons.

The information he held was vital in bringing Lady Langdale to justice. She was a villainous lady Colebourne had forced him to track for longer than he cared to. The duke had promised Falcone he would clear his debt once they captured the lady. Colebourne wanted her hung for her crimes against the good countrymen of England and every country she had spread her evil around.

Falcone grew weary of living under the duke's thumb and wished to leave this world behind. He wished to forge his own path, where he no longer spent his time following the duke's bidding. He had more than fulfilled his agreement with the duke. However, Colebourne thought otherwise.

Falcone cleared his throat, hoping the slight gesture would prompt the duke to state his demands so he could leave.

Colebourne continued to ignore Falcone. He meant to send a message to the marquess on who held the power in their dealings. He didn't like to display his authority in this manner, but Falcone had pushed his limits on the threat he made.

Colebourne held up the missive he had received yesterday from Barrett Ralston, his niece's husband. He had manipulated his leverage a few years ago when he forced Ralston to accept Falcone on his team to capture Lady Langdale. However, he now questioned if he should've kept Falcone committed to other dealings he was involved in. If Falcone followed through on his threat, then Colebourne would regret helping him keep his secrets.

Colebourne read the letter again.

A word of warning, Your man has information he threatens to expose if you don't force him to see the errors of his way.

Ralston didn't need to state who he referred to in the letter. Falcone. The gentleman who sat before him held the power to destroy his niece's family if he so chose. However, Colebourne still held his mark, allowing him full control over the marquess.

Colebourne glanced up, acknowledging Falcone for the first time. "Thank you for answering my request."

"You left me with no other choice," Falcone snarled.

Colebourne folded his hands together. "We all have choices, son. It is how we handle them that shows the depth of our character."

"I am not your son. Save your wisdom for him. Just state your orders so I can proceed with my day."

"You are aware of what I request of you. I would like your reassurance about how you will follow through with them."

Falcone leaned forward. "And if I do not? What then?"

Colebourne leaned back in his chair. "I believe you already know the answer to that, too."

Falcone scoffed. "I cannot win either way."

"It depends on how you see yourself as the champion."

Falcone blew out his breath, hoping it would help ease his irritation. However, it only built on the fury he tried to keep contained. "Enough with your philosophy. You leave me no choice but to remain silent. However, I will state how I no longer trust the Worthingtons. As soon as Dracott and Ravencroft betray them, I will bring them to justice right along with Lady Langdale. The debt I owe you and the destruction you will cause upon me will not matter."

Colebourne nodded. "Your warning is noted. You shall soon see how mistaken you are about Ravencroft and Dracott. They are victims of Lady Langdale's depravity and also wish for her demise. You would do well to heed my advice and work alongside them. They hold the knowledge of her organization and how to bring her to justice."

Falcone rose. "I'm never mistaken about a person's character, and those gentlemen are no different. I will promise you my silence for now."

Colebourne stood. "That is all I require of you." He held out his hand for Falcone to shake as a sign of good faith.

Falcone understood Colebourne's gesture for what it was. He stated his gentleman's promise to keep Falcone's secrets and expected him to do the same for his family. He had no other choice but to shake the duke's hand. Colebourne's firm grip displayed the most important message of all. Destroy his family and he would destroy everyone associated with him. Family. Friends. Acquaintances.

Colebourne would force Falcone to watch everyone suffer before he destroyed him.

Eden Worthington rocked the baby in her arms, smiling down at the sweet bundle. She loved babies with their intoxicating fragrance of sweet innocence. How they trusted so easily and their ability to adapt to an unfamiliar environment.

Eden struggled to adapt to the environment she was familiar with. It wasn't because she was unsure of herself or couldn't handle whatever situation she placed herself in. It was how she detested the underhanded, conniving, mean-spirited individuals she came across who required her to paste on a false smile and pretend she held no knowledge of their crimes. That was her reason for visiting her friend Jacqueline and rocking her newborn all afternoon. It helped to soothe her troubled soul.

Jacqueline placed the discarded toys on the shelf. "What troubles you today, my friend?"

Eden had met Jacqueline Kincaid after her brother Reese married Jacqueline's cousin Evelyn. When they met, they had both been unmarried ladies. However, after her uncle's matchmaking machinations, Jacqueline had married Griffen Kincaid, and they now had three children. The latest was an adorable little girl named Violet. Jacqueline had become one of Eden's dearest friends.

Eden slid her finger into the baby's grip. "Nothing. Can I not visit a friend and rock her newborn?"

Jacqueline laughed. "You are welcome whenever you please. However, this is your third visit this week. The excuses you state are to avoid your mother's pressure to get married. However, I believe something else troubles you."

Eden sighed. "Well, in my defense, the woman is relentless. Can you believe at the Seckington Ball last night she offered my hand to Lord Falcone to partner me in a quadrille?"

Jacqueline hid a smile behind her hand, not wishing to stir her friend's distress. "The audacity of her. Especially since Lord Falcone is an excellent dancer."

"He may be an excellent dancer, but he is the most annoying, exasperating gentleman I have ever had the misfortune of knowing."

"The manner in which you speak of the gentleman, one would wonder if you don't secretly harbor a tender for the marquess," Jacqueline teased.

Eden shuddered. "Even if he remained the last gentleman standing, I would never hold an ounce of affection for him."

Jacqueline took the baby from Eden's arms and settled her in the cradle. "I think you protest too strongly."

Eden scoffed. "He is an untrustworthy scoundrel who finds pleasure in tarnishing honorable gentlemen's character."

After covering her baby with a light blanket, Jacqueline sat on the window bench. "Who does he slander now?"

When the two ladies met Lord Falcone, Eden had never trusted him. However, Jacqueline had befriended the marquess, until he slandered Kincaid with false accusations involving Kincaid and Falcone's sister, who had married the Duke of Gostwicke. He had fled like the coward he was after he made his accusation. Which was the opinion Eden still held of the gentleman.

Jacqueline winced. "Before you answer that, I must confess something I should have years ago. However, it wasn't my story to tell. You need to understand Lord Falcone's declaration holds some truth behind it. While most is his perception of the circumstances, there is a sliver of facts that hold true."

Eden pinched her lips. "It doesn't matter. He should never have spoken over a matter that didn't involve him."

"It involved his sister. To defend her only speaks highly of the marquess's honor."

Eden didn't much care for how her friend defended the scoundrel's honor, even if she made a valid point. In truth, she preferred to hold the most discriminating of opinions about Falcone. Because if she acknowledged any of his finer characteristics, then she must admit to herself how his very presence affected her.

She refused to reflect on how his deep voice sent shivers of unexpected desire through her. How when he held her hand during their dance, her skin still tingled from his touch long after they parted. It left her suffering through a restless night, tossing and turning in bed, dreaming of how his kiss would feel.

Would his kiss be slow and gentle? Or would her senses unravel as they did whenever he was near? Even now, while they talked about Falcone, Eden fantasized about his kisses. As she had stated before, she found the gentleman infuriating.

"But what does it speak of his honor by threatening to expose our family's secrets for his revenge?" Eden countered.

Jacqueline frowned. "What is his threat?"

"To expose Ravencroft and Dracott's involvement with Lady Langdale's thievery ring. He doesn't trust them and believes they will betray our family in the end," Eden explained.

Eden trusted sharing this information with Jacqueline since she was family and Kincaid knew about Ravencroft's and Dracott's past with Lady Langdale. She only wished she could trust Falcone not to ruin her family.

"There is no need for you to worry," Jacqueline assured Eden.

"Yes, I must. I need to convince Graham to send Falcone off on another assignment. I still do not understand why the marquess works for him. Graham barely tolerates Falcone."

"It is best if Falcone stays in London. He holds valuable information on Lady L's crew. Also, Ralston and I can watch him," Griffen Kincaid spoke from the doorway.

"But there is no need for him since Ravencroft and Dracott have agreed to help destroy her," Eden argued.

Kincaid crossed the nursery and kissed Jacqueline. "Trust me, Eden. He is a valuable source we cannot afford to lose."

"Thank you for your advice, but I will speak with Graham on removing him from the case. It is the best solution for my family."

Jacqueline exchanged a look with her husband, urging him to tell her something concerning Lord Falcone.

Eden frowned. "What is it?"

"Tell her," Jacqueline urged. "She has a right to know since she works alongside him."

Kincaid pinched his lips, debating if he should tell Eden about the nature of Falcone's loyalty. He strode over to the window to stare outdoors while he decided if he should divulge the secret. He turned back to the ladies, where his wife tilted her head at Eden.

"What I am about to share with you cannot leave this room. It involves too many parties and will affect the dynamics in play," Kincaid started.

Eden nodded in understanding.

"A certain powerful duke has rescued many men and women from dire consequences. In repayment, he asks for their assistance to do his bidding until they clear their debts away."

"Are you implying Falcone in a sense works for the duke?" Eden asked.

"Yes," Kincaid answered.

"What does Colebourne hold on Falcone?" Eden wondered out loud. She would've laughed at the looks of shock on Jacqueline's and Kincaid's faces if they weren't discussing how Falcone could destroy her family with his sense of vengeance.

"How?" Kincaid muttered.

Eden quirked her eyebrow. "How do I know about Colebourne collecting people's debts to help his causes?"

Kincaid scoffed. "That is an elegant way of stating his biddings."

"I've heard rumors over the years within the family, and it appears Rogers, our butler, is indebted to Colebourne too."

"So then you understand . . ." Kincaid trailed off.

Eden nodded. Nothing more needed to be spoken on the subject. She didn't know why Kincaid had to repay a debt to Colebourne, nor was it any of her concern.

"Can Colebourne keep Falcone silent?" Eden inquired.

"For the time being, Falcone has promised Colebourne his loyalty. He would be a fool to cross him," Kincaid added.

"Well, fools have double-crossed for less," Eden mused.

Chapter Two

FALCONE WATCHED THE FLAXEN-HAIRED beauty stroll across the ballroom floor as if she were a queen. Eden Worthington carried her regal elegance with a confidence most men envied. And every gentleman she passed bowed down and pledged their undying devotion to her charms. A beauty every lady in attendance coveted for themselves.

Her ivory skin glowed under the candlelight, tempting him with the need he failed to restrain whenever she drew near. She wore her golden locks clasped behind her head with jeweled hair clips, and she had painted her plump lips red, a bold color for an unmarried lady. Her age may have reached past the debutante stage, but she was still young enough to cause the gossipmongers to whisper about her appearance.

As a pack of young pups surrounded her and begged her to partner with them for the next dance, her smile spread wide. Her teeth dug into her bottom lip as she tried to decide. He wanted to push his tongue against her teeth and soothe her lip, then dip inside and stroke against her tongue as he kissed her. Would her kiss be as bold as the lady herself?

He had fantasized over her for years, but he never wanted the trouble that accompanied the lady. Her sharp tongue was brutal enough to endure. Falcone only imagined what she'd reduce him to if he ever allowed himself to find out.

He held no clue what prompted him to set out across the ballroom. However, he found himself amongst the pups, pushing his way to her side. "Scamper away. Lady Eden has already promised the next dance to me."

With many disgruntled groans, they followed his command, and he was alone with the lady. However, she didn't wear a pleased expression at being rescued from the young gentlemen. Her usual snarl whenever she encountered him twisted her lips. Why had he intervened?

"I am not aware I have promised you a single thing, Lord Falcone."

Even the sound of her voice was a soft melody to his ears. God. He needed to either bed this lady or find a mistress to keep him occupied from the immoral thoughts he held of her.

Because each thought held more decadence than the last. Each one was filled with reaching the pinnacle of satisfaction he would only find between her thighs. No lady had ever controlled his every thought like her.

Falcone tried to charm her. "You wouldn't want to make a fool of me, would you?"

"It wouldn't take much to make a fool of you," Eden snarled.

Yes. He definitely wanted to kiss that snarl from her lips. Even her smart quips at his character amused him. She was a fiery vixen who inflamed his desire by her mere presence alone.

He turned. "I never figured you for a coward."

Eden hissed an unladylike growl at the irritating marquess who disrupted her perfect evening with his appearance. To think she needed to be rescued. Pshh. Falcone ruined the attention she received from the young bucks as they flattered her gloomy ego. She wanted to stomp her feet at the unfairness of life throwing this gentleman in her path at every opportunity, when she only wanted to avoid him.

She gritted her teeth and slipped her arm through his before he wandered too far away. "I am no coward, and you are no gentleman."

"I never professed I was," Falcone whispered in her ear.

Before she responded, the haunting melody of a waltz began. She didn't realize when she responded to his taunt what dance she would have to share with him. The intimacy of a waltz held a seductive spell that made one want to succumb to their desires. Dancing close to Falcone would stir those desires to life. Desires she must resist.

His whisper in her ear caused her to shiver, and she tried to calm herself, but her body betrayed her by trembling. Her fingers shook in his hand, and her heart quickened when his dark gaze scrutinized her with each turn around the floor. She waited for a comment from him stating his observations, but he remained quiet.

While dancing with a silent Eden was quite peaceful, he also found it quite dull. He much preferred the sharp tongue slicing through his character than this demure dance partner.

A wicked smile lifted his lips. "Did their attention make you feel young again?"

A blush spread across her cheeks, and her eyes snapped at him. "I do not deserve your insult."

He shrugged in time with the music. "'Tis not meant as an insult. I only stated the obvious."

"You atrocious reprobate," Eden sputtered.

"Now who is insulting whom? Is your mother aware of your vulgar tongue?" Falcone asked with innocence.

Eden glared at him. "My mother would approve of how I set you in your proper place."

He bent his head to whisper again. "And where exactly is my proper place? Perhaps underneath the bedsheets with you?"

Eden gasped and stopped dancing, her mouth opening and closing like a fish. The lord was a scoundrel for expressing such a scandalous suggestion. He held no honorable morals.

Usually, he would have taken pleasure in silencing her. Who knew a crass suggestion would utter her speechless? If so, he would've attempted this method before. However, they drew the other dancers' attention, and soon the entire ballroom would whisper of Eden's actions.

Falcone wrapped his arms around Eden's waist and whisked her into a twirl, right out onto the terrace. He glanced over his shoulder and noted how no one saw them leave. He moved them deeper into the shadows.

Eden swatted at his grip. "Unhand me, you brute."

Falcone chuckled, pulling her tighter against him. "No. I do not believe I will."

Heat invaded him at the brush of her soft curves pressed against him. Her breasts swelled against her dress with each agitated breath she drew. Falcone wanted to draw his tongue along the crease where the globes pushed together and trail a path down the valley between them until he reached her nipples. He would take long, slow licks across the tips before drawing them between his lips. Would she whimper or moan with her passionate need?

The longer she allowed him to hold her in an intimate embrace, the further Eden sank into the unknown. However, she was powerless to resist him, no matter how much she argued with herself about how highly improper their embrace was. She saw how his eyes glazed over with desire as he stared at her breasts.

"You barbaric neanderthal, release me now! How dare you apprehend me and ruin my reputation with your bold advances. I will make sure you—"

Eden never had the chance to finish her threat because Falcone captured her mouth under his. His kiss struck her unaware and left her not only speechless but awakened by the fiery licks of his tongue caressing her lips to open. His tongue invaded her mouth with bold strokes against hers. Eden whimpered at the sinfully delicious taste of him.

While he had fantasized about kissing Eden, he never meant to. However, he didn't know any other way to silence her attack on his character. With each comment, her snarl had increased. And he had wanted nothing more than to kiss her ruby-red lips into silence. Her whimpers answered his question, yet he hungered to hear her moans of pleasure.

Eden clung to Falcone in her attempt to save herself from drowning. Her hands slid up his chest, and her fingers scrunched up his lapels as she anchored herself against him. His firm muscles protected her from the brutal waves of desire washing over her and provided her with a false sense of protection. Because his very kiss weighed her down in an ocean of doubt over his intentions toward her. And left her wondering why she even responded to his kiss.

He meant to quiet her with his kiss, but with each lick, he never wanted to stop. She clung to him as she returned him kiss for kiss. She tasted like the cheap champagne she drank mixed with her own sweetness, and he wished to savor more of the unique flavor.

But he must stop this madness or else he would find himself a groom to this infuriating lady. Or exiled from England. Her connection to Colebourne was enough to make him regain his sanity and pull away from her. He peeled her fingers off his suit coat and leaned back against the wall.

He swiped his thumb over his lips, wiping away her lip color. The red stain flashed a warning at him about how he should keep his distance from her. However, he had never been one to avoid a challenge, and Eden Worthington was a challenge he found amusing to toy with.

He pulled out his handkerchief and wiped away the lip color from his thumb. "If I had known a simple kiss would halt your insults, I could've enjoyed the silence sooner over the last few years."

When she shook herself out of her daze, Eden reacted by sheer instinct and nothing else. The state of her confusion about what had just transpired forced her to strike out. She lifted her hand to slap him across the face, but Falcone caught her wrist, stopping her. He tightened his grip when she tried to tug it free.

"You seem to have a problem of keeping your hands to yourself this evening, Lord Falcone. Is this how you get a lady to fall victim to your charms? By manhandling her?"

He jerked her back against his chest and whispered, "Do not take your frustrations out on me for enjoying the kiss we shared. You only have yourself to blame for responding. No force was necessary on my part to draw out your whimpers of enjoyment."

He released her and took up his stance against the wall again. Eden stood before him in a state of fury, piercing him with her fiery gaze as if she held the capability to burn him on the spot. She was a glorious vixen with her pent-up frustration, set out to destroy him by tempting him to forgo his senses, to fall at her feet in worship.

Eden lost the ability to form a reply to his taunt. Because, in all honesty, every word he spoke was true. Still, her hand itched to slap the smirk off his handsome face. Why was he so irritatingly attractive?

She clutched her skirts and hurried away, escaping the need to throw herself at him for another scandalous kiss. The gentleman tempted her to forget every rational thought she still possessed.

Eden slipped back inside, her absence going unnoticed. While working for her brother Graham, she had learned how to move about a ballroom floor inconspicuously. At first she had had difficulty because every gentleman found themselves infatuated with her beauty. They had clamored to her side, begging for a dance. However, they were unprepared for the beauty to hold opinions on a variety of topics. Eden wasn't one to shy away from a conversation if she found it unpleasant. She would state her opinion, and they would scurry away, never to return.

Which left her free to wander, seeking the information Graham needed for his cases. She found it much more pleasurable than pretending interest in a gentleman to gain an offer of marriage. Eden had no plans to marry, even after watching her two sisters marry their soul mates.

Eden clung to her cynicism about how not everyone had a soul mate waiting for them. If so, she had yet to meet hers and had no inclination to search for him. No. She enjoyed the life she lived and didn't wish for it to be any different.

Eden found her family mingled in with the Duke of Colebourne's family, talking amongst themselves. Jacqueline winked at her before continuing her conversation with Eden's sister Noel.

"I saw you dancing with Lord Falcone. Why did he not return you to our side? Did you have a spat with him again?" Lady Worthington asked her daughter.

Eden's cheeks grew warm with a blush as she remembered how they more than danced. "Now why does the blame lie at fault with me since he didn't escort me back to my family? Do you imagine the boar has an inkling of proper behavior? The gentleman needs taught manners of proper decorum."

"Perhaps that should be you, my dear," Lady Worthington suggested.

Eden shuddered. "I believe I shall leave that misfortune to another lady who deserves the likes of Lord Falcone."

Colebourne chuckled. "My, you hold a harsh opinion of the gentleman."

Eden tilted her head. "If you consider Falcone a gentleman, then you have set your requirements for one very low."

The duke gave her a shrewd gaze before changing the subject. "Now that your mother has married off your sisters, will you walk down the aisle next or is Graham that lucky soul?"

Eden wagged her finger at him. "Do not even think of playing matchmaker with me. I want no part of your drama."

Colebourne drew the flute to his lips to hide his smile. "I would never dream of it."

Eden smiled because she could never stay cross with the duke. "See that you don't."

"Excuse me, Lady Eden."

Eden turned to find one of the young gentlemen from earlier standing behind her. "Yes?"

"I wondered if you would enjoy a dance now?"

"A wonderful idea." Eden slipped her hand onto his offered arm.

Eden jumped at the opportunity to get away from her mother pushing Falcone at her as a potential groom. Her mother wouldn't if she knew how he threatened to ruin their family by spilling their secrets. Also, she thought it was only fair to dance with the gentleman since Falcone had scared him off earlier. Now if only she could remember his name.

It didn't matter because he was only a means of escape. And perhaps he could help her forget the dance she had shared with Falcone, one that would surely fill her dreams. Or should she say nightmares? Either way, the gentleman's dancing ability didn't compare to the smooth grace with which Falcone had led them across the dance floor. Nor did the gentleman's touch make her quiver and long for him to steal her onto the terrace. A sense of loneliness for a certain marquess washed over Eden as she danced.

The very same marquess watched Eden dance with the bumbling fool he had stolen her away from earlier. The bloke couldn't even count the damn steps and kept stepping on Eden's slippers. He wanted to laugh at her expense, but instead he fought the demon of jealousy nipping at him. Falcone wanted to stroll onto the dance floor and interrupt their dance. And do what? He sure as hell didn't want to give her family any ideas of his interest. No. His interest in Eden only consisted of them between the bedsheets. Hell, he didn't even require a bed with how he desired to scandalize her.

A wicked grin spread across his face at how he would seek his revenge against Colebourne for forcing him to keep his silence. What better way to endure his sentence than to seduce the flaxen-haired beauty?

"Do you think it is a possibility?" Lady Worthington murmured, watching her daughter dance.

Colebourne surveyed them as well. "Anything is a possibility, my dear Meredith. Are you prepared to undertake the task, considering what the gentleman has questioned?"

Lady Worthington turned toward Colebourne. "He only makes those threats because he follows protocol and tries to act honorable. It is our actions that are questionable."

Colebourne nodded. "Then shall we?"

Lady Worthington glanced across the ballroom and saw Lord Falcone staring at her daughter. His blatant arousal was more than obvious. A devious smile lit her face at the plans she had in store to bring them together. A spark against a flame led to the most explosive sight to gaze upon. And they were two souls who needed their souls to ignite.

"We shall."

Chapter Three

EDEN PRESSED HER EAR against the closed door, hoping to overhear the heated argument between Falcone and Ralston. But she couldn't make out a single word. During one part of the discussion, she heard one gentleman pound on the wall in frustration. Darn her brother for installing such a thick door. It made it impossible to hear anything of importance.

"Perhaps if you turn the knob and walk in, it might help with your eavesdropping," Graham spoke behind her, scaring her enough to let out a squeak.

The argument went silent after her little yelp. She turned, annoyed with her brother for disturbing her. Even though she was clearly at fault.

"They locked the door," Eden informed Graham.

"Well, of course they did. It is what one does when they require privacy," Graham quipped.

He didn't wait for her reply but knocked twice, followed by a pause, then three more knocks. It was a code Ralston had devised to convey they waited for entrance.

Ralston opened the door and ushered them inside. He smiled at Eden as she sat on the sofa. Falcone leaned against the wall with an air of indifference. The fury he had expressed with Ralston earlier was now hidden behind a calm mask.

Worth sat behind his desk. "Have you gentlemen come to a compromise and settled the differences interfering with our investigation?"

Ralston glared at Falcone. "We are at an impasse, but Falcone has agreed to remain silent. Until something jeopardizes the investigation or if we risk his life. He stated, 'Then life can go to hell, but I will speak my mind.'"

Worth nodded. "Fair enough. Now let us discuss our next plan of action."

"Should we not wait for Dracott and Ravencroft?" Eden asked.

Worth avoided his sister's eyes. "No. This will only involve you and Falcone."

"How so?" Eden's gaze darted at Falcone, but he continued acting indifferent.

Worth shuffled the papers on his desk, uncomfortable with what he must ask of his sister. However, it was vital to their case for her to agree. He only hoped Reese didn't catch wind of the party they needed Eden to attend. If Reese or their mother discovered their plans, they would forbid Eden from working with his agency again.

Ralston sat at his desk and propped his feet on the edge, finding amusement in his partner's discomfort. "Would you like me to give them the details?"

Worth grimaced. "Would you?"

Ralston laughed. "With pleasure." He looked at Eden and then at Falcone. "In four days, Lord Chesterton and his bride will host a masquerade party to celebrate their Gretna Green nuptials. We have secured both of you invitations to the sinful event."

Falcone pushed off the wall. "No!"

Falcone's firm denial made Eden leery to question what they required of them to attend the party. How was it even possible for her to attend? "Mama will never give her permission."

"You are not so innocent to believe that Worth would obtain your mother's permission to attend a party of debauchery, are you?" Falcone smirked.

Eden blushed. Actually, she was naïve and held no clue about the worldly sins the ton took part in. For Falcone to believe otherwise explained their kiss from the other evening. The very kiss she couldn't stop dreaming of, even now when his lips moved with his displeasure at their plan. She couldn't focus on his words because she wondered if he would ever attempt to kiss her again.

"Eden? Eden?" Ralston's voice drifted into her fantasy.

She shook her head to clear her thoughts. "Sorry. What did you ask?"

"If you were comfortable with attending?" Ralston asked again.

"You cannot mean to whore out your sister?" Falcone ranted.

Eden kept her gaze lowered. "What is required of me?"

Falcone's insistence on keeping them from attending the party heightened her curiosity. Was it as sinful as he made it sound? If so, how?

Ralston dropped his feet to the floor and leaned across his desk. "Your attendance is only for the benefit of watching for anything suspicious. We have information the bride is a member of Lady L's gang and she has enticed Lord Chesterton to host a party filled with sinful temptations. We believe Lady L's gang will use this party as a dress rehearsal for their big heist. Since we ruined her plans with the extra security at Ravencroft and Noel's wedding, she has devised new plans. Anything you overhear will help our case."

"But won't they know who I am and keep me from entering?" Eden asked.

"A slight change in your appearance will help to disguise who you are. Plus, you will wear a mask the entire time. The invitation is for a Lady Palmer," Ralston explained.

Eden nodded at Falcone. "And what is his alias?"

"Falcone will go as himself," Worth stated.

Eden crinkled her brows in confusion. "But won't Lady L's crew recognize him?"

Worth smirked at Falcone, enjoying what he was about to say. "Yes, they will. But they will think he has returned to his wicked habits. Because over the next few days, Lord Falcone will fall victim to his corrupt vices again, leaving everyone to question where his loyalties lie. Especially since he has shown his displeasure with us lately."

They had him pressed against a wall and found pleasure in it. He had no choice but to follow their orders. Colebourne had made sure of that. But it wasn't only their demands that made him agree. It was the spark shining from Eden's eyes as they described what was required of her. He didn't know if her enthusiasm was from the chance they gave her to contribute to the investigation, instead of the measly tasks they usually assigned her. Or if attending a sinful party sparked her interest. Either way, he must agree, if only to protect Eden from every scoundrel in attendance.

He wanted to throttle Worth for suggesting Eden attend the party. However, he also wanted to express his gratitude for gifting him the chance to seduce his sister. The masquerade party was an excellent opportunity to tempt Eden with the many pleasurable delights they might partake in.

"Very clever of you to consider every aspect of this plan to guarantee my allegiance," Falcone snarled. He would allow them to assume they controlled him. When, in fact, once this ordeal ended, he would seek his freedom and no one would control him again.

Ralston shrugged. "We must finish this investigation, and your role is nothing more than a professional obligation. We're all after the same goal: to bring Lady L to justice. If some of us must sacrifice our well-standing name to reach our objective, then so be it."

"So you're willing to sacrifice your sister's standing in society to move ahead in the world?" Falcone asked Worth.

Worth stood and crossed to the window. "No one will know it is Eden because you will never leave her side. They will assume you have brought along a paramour to indulge the evening with."

Worth stared outside, understanding how Falcone judged him. It wasn't his finest moment, but their options were limited. Dracott's source had relayed the information about the party. Before Lady L struck again and wreaked havoc on anyone else, they needed to gain intelligence and capture her. Eden was levelheaded, and her intelligence would keep her protected. Also, he had no other choice. He must trust Falcone to protect her, too. Colebourne swore by the man.

Worth had approached the duke to inquire the reason behind Falcone's debt to him. Colebourne wouldn't disclose the reason, but he had informed Worth how Falcone had led a different lifestyle in the past. It hadn't taken Worth long to learn about Falcone's past when he questioned the correct people. However, Colebourne had also stated how much he trusted Falcone and stressed how they needed to place their faith in the marquess and hope Falcone didn't betray them in the end.

"Do both of you agree?" Ralston asked.

Gemma strolled into the office. "Agree to what?" Gemma kissed Ralston on the cheek, then turned to smile at everyone.

He stood up and gave a slight shake of his head for everyone to keep silent. "Nothing, my dear."

Gemma noted the uncomfortable silence. "Obviously it is something considering your serious expressions. Does this concern Lady Langdale? Selina told me how vicious the lady can be. Did you know Lady L threatened to expose Selina and Duncan over a kiss they shared while she was engaged to Lucas? And remember that family heirloom she stole, Barrett? I hope you capture her soon. She is an evilness we do not need in society."

Eden laughed, breaking the tension. "That is our plan."

"Excellent. Are you ready, my dear?" Gemma smiled at her husband.

Ralston bowed to his wife before wrapping his arm around her waist. "I am always ready for you, my love."

Ralston swept Gemma toward the door but paused at the threshold. He glanced over his shoulder with his eyebrow quirked, waiting for their answers.

"Yes," Eden agreed.

Falcone scowled. They left him with no other choice but to agree. "Yes."

No sooner than the Ralstons had left, Worth muttered something incoherent and swiftly departed, leaving Eden alone with Falcone. He stared at her as if he tried to understand her. She was aware of how it appeared when she accepted the task with eagerness. He thought it was because of her curiosity. When really, it gave her a sense of pride at how they trusted her to handle a complicated assignment.

Not wanting Falcone to realize how uneasy he made her, she tilted her head to the side and observed him in the same manner. "What were they referring to when they mentioned your old vices?"

Falcone stood up straight. "That is none of your concern."

Eden rose. She felt exposed sitting there, vulnerable to his response to her curiosity. "It should be, considering we are to be partners."

Falcone scoffed. "We are not partners. You are the distraction that will snare everyone's attention away from what my motives are for attending a party filled with the degenerate members of the ton."

Eden's eyebrow arched. "From the sounds of it, you were once one of those degenerates."

Falcone stalked over to her. "You have no clue."

Eden shuffled towards the door, but Falcone beat her to it. He closed the door and blocked her path by leaning against it. "Running away again?"

Eden lifted her chin. "No. I am only leaving because it is inappropriate for us to be alone."

Falcone took two steps toward her. "Yet we shall soon be left alone where no one can rescue you."

She tried to step around him, but Falcone moved as if they were dancing. He made her feel like a mouse trying to outsmart a cat as he toyed with her for his amusement. Somehow, she lost the ability to counterattack his taunts. If she couldn't voice how he held no effect over her senses, then she must act as nonchalantly as he did.

Eden pulled on her gloves and motioned for him to move. "If you do not mind, Lord Falcone, I must leave."

He stepped but a breath apart from her. "But I do mind, Lady Eden."

Falcone enjoyed watching her squirm. Did their kiss unsettle her? He tucked a stray curl behind her ear and gazed at her trembling lips. Did she ache to share a kiss again, as he did? How would she taste today?

He bent his head. "I mind very much," Falcone whispered before brushing his lips across hers.

The soft touch of his lips was a contradiction to the tension surrounding them. Why was he disturbed by Worth's proposal and how easily she agreed to it? Perhaps he was an honorable gentleman like her mother stated. But would an honorable gentleman kiss an unmarried lady?

His lips coaxed her mouth open and drew her into a deep kiss. The soft stroke of his tongue moved alongside hers in a slow dance. Eden gripped her reticule, fighting the urge to wrap her arms around his neck and draw him in closer. If she had imagined the kiss they shared the other evening dominated her senses, it held nothing to the slow seduction of this kiss.

Falcone savored the hint of cherries on her tongue. It only made his hunger for her intensify. He wanted more than to kiss her. Falcone wanted to lay her on the sofa and worship every inch of her. He desired to show her how scandalous his past was. It filled him with disgust now, but at the time, he had enjoyed the many sinful delights. Especially from innocent misses like Eden.

He stepped back. Eden would soon learn of his past lifestyle. If Worth and Ralston meant to force him back into it, then he would reap the benefits. Graham Worthington held no idea how he sacrificed his sister, but Falcone would enjoy every single debaucherous second of it.

Falcone swept his arm out. "I am done minding. You may leave."

Eden's eyes flashed open to see a smirk of satisfaction spread across Falcone's face. "You are an irritating, infuriating arse."

Eden didn't wait for him to comment and stormed out of the office. However, his laughter followed her clear out to the carriage. In her frustration, she didn't see Graham walking in her path. Her brother's distraction caught her attention, and she swept Falcone's kiss from her mind.

Graham almost plowed into Eden. "I am sorry, dear sister. My thoughts were elsewhere."

Eden frowned. "Yes, I noticed. Why did you leave so suddenly?"

Graham looked over his shoulder, searching the street. But whoever or whatever he searched for he must not have found. "I thought I saw someone familiar, but they disappeared before I reached them."

"Who was it?"

Graham shook his head. "No one important." He helped her into the carriage and settled on the opposite seat.

Eden set her reticule next to her. "Are you returning home for lunch?"

Graham gathered her hands into his. "No. I must get back inside the office. I only wanted to talk with you privately. If we overstepped our bounds by our request, say so now and we shall forget we ever asked you. It is a solid plan, and I knew we could depend on you. However, if working closely with Falcone will bother you or if the party is too shocking, we can devise another plan."

Eden squeezed his hands. "No. I am honored you trust me enough for such a daunting task."

"And Falcone?"

"Pshh. I can handle the marquess. Do not worry, dear brother."

Graham nodded, satisfied with Eden's answer. "This must stay between us. You cannot breathe a word to anyone other than Falcone and Ralston."

Eden sat back in the seat. "I am aware of what a secret mission entails."

Graham climbed out of the carriage. "Excellent. We shall finalize the details tomorrow. I shall see you at dinner."

Graham directed the driver to take Eden home. She stared out the window and wondered what Falcone had in store for her. She may be as naïve as he stated, but she was also a woman who sensed the marquess would attempt a seduction at the scandalous masquerade party.

The only question was whether she would allow Falcone to seduce her.

Chapter Four

EDEN DUG THROUGH THE wardrobe for a dress she might alter for the masquerade party. However, none would work. She needed a revealing dress to fit the part she would play. Also one that would tempt Falcone to ravish her lips.

As much as he had infuriated her today, the attraction still pulled at her. Especially when he had displayed his honorable intentions by trying to convince Graham and Ralston that the party wasn't appropriate for her to attend. A part of her heart had thawed. However, his mocking words had frozen it back into place.

Her heart had melted all over again after he kissed her. Eden sat on the bed, staring at her demure dresses. She wondered if only Falcone ignited a fire in her soul or if any gentleman could.

She had felt out of sorts since her sisters found happiness and married for love. Eden didn't envy them. If a man showed his devotion toward her, would she find happiness? She wanted a man to hold an uncontrollable passion for her but still give her the freedom to pursue her interests.

While Falcone had declared his desire, his actions today showed he wouldn't allow her any pursuits. Not that she considered him a possible groom. The gentleman was a thorn in her side she dealt with when needed, which unfortunately would be in a few nights. Perhaps if she tempted him, she might have the chance to explore her sexuality.

He had introduced her to passion, and since she didn't wish to wed, perhaps she might take a lover. Falcone was the perfect gentleman to teach her the ways of lovemaking. He would want nothing beyond a tumble. Eden could keep her freedom and continue helping Graham with his causes.

Her sisters strolled into her bedchamber as she hung the dresses back in the wardrobe.

"What are you doing?" Maggie asked.

"Nothing," Eden mumbled.

Noel looked between the wardrobe and the dresses spread out across the bed. "It doesn't appear like nothing."

"Well, it is." Eden continued putting the dresses away.

Noel lifted a dress, pressed it against her, and looked at it in the mirror. She switched from side to side, crinkling her nose at how the color washed her skin out. "Are you looking for a dress to impress Lord Falcone?"

Eden grabbed the dress out of Noel's hands. "Now, why would I care what Lord Falcone sees me in?"

Noel and Maggie exchanged a look, then snickered. Eden rolled her eyes at them.

"Perhaps because you wish to draw his eyes toward you," Noel stated.

Maggie bounced on the bed. "Noel is under the impression that Lord Falcone is your destiny. Ravencroft is skeptical and doesn't agree with her. So she has recruited me to see if you find him desirable. So do you?"

Eden gasped. "How ridiculous. Of course I don't."

Noel clapped her hands together. "She protests with haste."

Eden shook her head in exasperation. "Has marriage addled your ability to comprehend? I said I was not. How much clearer must I be about Lord Falcone? He is the most exasperating gentleman who has ever graced my presence."

Noel's lips lifted into a dreamy smile. "My marriage is divine, just like my husband. Ravencroft may have the ability to make me lose my train of thought, but I still hold the ability to understand how my sister denies her feelings for a certain lord."

"I do not deny anything but state the cold, hard facts of how I view Lord Falcone."

Maggie laid back against the pillows. "I thought you two made a handsome couple the other night during your dance. However, one aspect of the dance I didn't understand."

Eden frowned, unsure of what Maggie referred to. "And that was?"

"Where did the two of you disappear to?"

"You never told me about that part," Noel accused.

"I thought I would spring it on you. I know how you love the flair for the dramatic. And what better drama than wondering where our sister had wandered off to with the *divine* marquess? Am I using the word divine correctly?" Maggie teased Noel.

Noel tilted her head in approval. "Yes, quite so." She turned to Eden. "Do share with us, sister. Where did you and the *divine* marquess disappear to?"

Nosy, busybody sisters who wouldn't mind their own business. She refused to tell them how divine the marquess actually was. Well, he was only divine when he kissed her. Otherwise he was as irritating as them. However, they must never get a whiff of how she melted at his kisses, yearned for his caress, and desired for him to make love to her. If they discovered her secret, they would become as relentless as their mother in manipulating them together at every opportunity that presented itself.

Eden gave her sisters an annoyed look. "You are imagining things. Falcone and I never left the dance floor. You must have lost sight of us among the other dancers. He mumbled some excuse and abandoned me on the other side of the ballroom. Like I stated before, the marquess does not qualify to be called a gentleman."

Noel huffed. "I had hoped to hear how the marquess stole a kiss."

Maggie sat back up and folded her legs underneath her, wearing a smirk that didn't bode well for Eden. "Perhaps he did and Eden is too quick to deny it."

Noel joined Maggie on the bed, her eyes alight. "Do go on."

"Margaret Ann," Eden warned.

Maggie's smirk widened. "Well, Crispin and I stood near the terrace doors at the end of the dance and saw Eden rushing inside over to Mama. Not soon after, Lord Falcone strutted in, appearing quite smug." Maggie paused for a dramatic effect. "And his lips wore a shade of red lip color."

Noel gasped and swung her gaze over to Eden. She had fought back from blushing at their first mention of Falcone, but with Maggie divulging her gossip, a flood of warmth overtook Eden and she lowered herself onto the divan and tried to avoid her sisters' curiosity.

"Didn't Eden wear red lip color?" Noel asked.

"Yes. The same exact shade Lord Falcone wore for the rest of the ball," Maggie quipped.

Noel laughed. "Oh! I knew it."

"You know nothing," Eden growled.

"Well, your blush proves that Lord Falcone did indeed kiss you. You protest too loudly of your denials toward the marquess. The only question is, why?"

"Why what?" Eden asked in exasperation.

Noel held a secretive smile. "Only you understand. Come along, Maggie, we promised Mama our help."

Maggie jumped off the bed. "If you want my opinion, I believe you and Falcone would make an excellent couple."

"He makes threats against our family. Have both of you forgotten that slight matter?"

Maggie shrugged. "I do not believe he will, and neither does Crispin."

"Gregory holds the same opinion. Deny it all you want, but Falcone is your soul mate," Noel added.

Eden scoffed. "There is no such thing as soul mates."

Maggie and Noel regarded her with saddened expressions. Did they feel sorry for her? They would leave her wondering since neither of them offered a rebuttal to her comment.

Before they left, Maggie turned to her. "Just a word of warning. Mama holds the same impression of how Lord Falcone is the perfect gentleman for you. I heard her consorting with Colebourne on playing matchmaker."

Eden leapt off the divan and started toward them. "That isn't what you agreed to help Mama with, is it?" She followed them into the hallway. "Noel? Maggie?"

Her sisters never answered her but continued on their way, giggling at her demise. Noel had corrupted Maggie or else her marriage to Dracott had made her soft. Maggie never giggled like a lady. If they had enticed Maggie to their side, then her list of allies to remain single dwindled away. Which only left Graham to help keep her from falling victim to the Marriage Mart. They were all fools anyhow. Falcone might present himself as a marriageable gentleman, but Eden knew for a fact he was a scoundrel. One who would seduce her and then stroll away without another glance. That was perfectly fine with her.

Or was it?

For the past two nights, Falcone had immersed himself in his former life, and it had welcomed him with open arms. But then again, the ton's debauchery wasn't picky about who it allowed to take part in the vices of their decadent sins.

His depraved cohorts from a lifetime ago still frequented the same establishments, singing their approval. They would spread word of his return. Before long, Lady Langdale would entice him to join her world. That was the key goal of his current assignment, not the masquerade party. Oh, the party remained a crucial part of the plan, but not the one to secure him an offer from Lady Langdale. It was a diversion to keep him in line, as well as for Ralston and Worth to state who held the ultimate power.

He rocked his chair back onto two legs and leaned against the wall. With his lids lowered, he perused the room. He took a draw on his cigar and followed it with a long pull from the bottle of whiskey he held in his lap. Women of every shape and size, wearing sheer negligees that left nothing to the imagination, wandered the room to find their conquest for the night. Most were barely out of the schoolroom, and the others were past their prime. They remained because they had no other opportunity to survive elsewhere.

In the past, Falcone had spread his favors amongst them, sharing his skills as a lover to teach them how to make more coin. He had taken pleasure in teaching an innocent how to suck his cock and enjoy the delights of a ménage. He found the most thrill when he fed their addictions to where they craved the decadent lifestyle as much as the depraved souls who frequented this establishment. Taking their innocence and twisting them into soulless creatures had become a game to appease his boredom.

Until that fateful night where his life had changed forever. A night he could never undo and one that tormented his soul with the horrors of his destruction.

He would repent for his sins by permitting them to force him back into this hell, only for the sake of destroying the most evilness of them all.

A hand trailed down his chest, across his stomach, and straight to his cock. He grabbed her wrist before her hand palmed him. His lids raised, and he took in the girl in front of him. She held the innocence of youth, but the circumstances life had dealt her left her with a jaded expression. At one time, he would have leapt at the chance of corrupting her further. Now, sickness settled in his gut. However, he must never allow it to rule his actions. He must pretend that he had fallen back into his old vices.

His grip loosened, and he rubbed his thumb across her wrist, watching her expression change to one of greed. For a brief second, he pitied her, but now he only held disgust toward her. A person who needed coin for survival and a person who wanted coin for wealth expressed themselves differently. And this girl fell into the latter category. However, he would use her for his end.

His chair landed on all fours, and he pulled her between his legs. She dropped to her knees and skated her hands between his thighs. Her lashes fluttered at him. "Some girls mentioned how you can teach a girl certain skills."

Her touch left him cold, but he needed to play along for appearance's sake. He pulled her hair back behind her shoulders, then trailed his fingers lightly across her cheek. "And what skills might those be, sweetness?"

Her fingers toyed with the buttons on the placket of his trousers. "The different ways to suck a cock to ensure a gentleman will keep returning."

His thumb dug into her bottom lip. "I am sure this mouth already holds the skills for that."

Her tongue licked across his thumb, drawing it into her mouth. "I need more practice and a more skillful teacher."

Perhaps the girl held more innocence than he thought. Because his cock lay inside his trousers, soft and unresponsive to her seduction. He cringed at her blatant display of wickedness, and he didn't understand why, but guilt settled over him. All he imagined in this young girl's place was Eden Worthington instead. Why did he hold remorse for playing a part that Ralston and Worth demanded of him? He owed Eden nothing. If he wanted, he could indulge for old time's sake by teaching the girl how to suck his cock properly and then plow into her. Perhaps it would wipe away every single thought of the lady who had snuck into his conscience. Instead of his cock hardening, it remained the same. Soft and uninterested.

He took another pull from his cigar and tapped the ashes onto the floor right next to her. "The gentlemen who fill this parlor are more than willing to teach you."

She undid a button. "But none as skilled as you."

He allowed her to unbutton two more. "You want my coin to learn a new skill? That seems unfair. What will you offer in exchange?"

The girl sat back with confusion when he buttoned his trousers. "But . . . I . . ."

Falcone stood above her. "I am sure you also heard the advice of how I give nothing away for free. I expect a favor in return."

After he took two steps away, she quickly gave him the answer he wanted. "Anything. I will do anything you require of me."

Falcone turned, holding out his hand to help her rise. "Excellent. Your name, my dear?"

"Melody."

"Come along, Melody, you have much to learn this evening." Falcone wrapped his arm around Melody's waist and led her up the stairs to a private bedchamber he had requested for the evening.

He didn't miss the gloating look Melody sent to the other ladies in the welcoming parlor as he escorted her out. She plastered herself to his side, engulfing him in the musky aroma of a prostitute. He held no recourse for dragging her into the middle of his chaos because she was the type of person who scented it out and planted herself firmly within its grasp.

He only hoped his choice wouldn't be his demise.

Chapter Five

E DEN TUGGED ON THE gown, trying to cover her displayed
bosom. She stared at herself in the mirror, unsure if she
had the nerve to attend the party. The gown hugged her every
curve, leaving nothing to a man's imagination. The neckline
of the gown sat decadently low. One wrong move and she
would spill out of the gown. Her nipples rested underneath the
decorative trim. The skirt held slits along each side so her legs
were on full display with each step she took. Her arms were
bare, except for the assortment of bracelets adorning them.
A necklace hung from her neck, holding a ruby pendant that
dipped in and out of the valley of her breasts at her every
movement.

She had brushed her hair into an assortment of waves,
with curls dangling down her back. The softness of her hair
caressed her bare shoulders when she swished her head back
and forth. She had refused to wear the dress when she saw
how the gown displayed her attributes. However, she had to
admit how fascinating the creation was after she stared at the
creature in the mirror.

"Lord Falcone will find himself unable to resist you this
evening. I predict he will not stop with a single kiss this time,"
Gemma declared.

Jacqueline's eyes widened. "This time? Has Lord Falcone and Eden shared a kiss before?"

Eden frowned at her friends. When Graham and Ralston made her promise to stay silent about the masquerade party, it had only pertained to the ladies in her family. The gentlemen knew she would require help in dressing for the part, so Ralston and Kincaid had enlisted their wives. Kincaid had men planted at the party to protect her. Also, her friends helped to provide an excuse for her absence without her mother questioning her motives.

Eden lifted the container holding the lip paint and twisted off the lid. "You have talked with Noel."

Gemma's eyes twinkled. "And Maggie."

Eden groaned. Gemma's answer supplied proof of Maggie's defection since she indulged in gossip. Eden painted her lips instead of defending herself. She pulled her lips into a pout, making sure she didn't miss a spot.

"I think Falcone would approve, especially if you keep your lips just so," Gemma continued.

Jacqueline cleared her throat. "Do you care to clue me in?"

"Maggie noticed Eden and Lord Falcone disappear during their dance and then later saw them return from the terrace. Falcone was wearing a trace of red lip color," Gemma gushed.

"The same red lip color our friend is wearing now?" Jacqueline inquired.

Gemma nodded.

Jacqueline smiled. "Eden, do you have anything to refute this gossip?"

Eden added the lip color to her reticule. "I never trouble myself with gossip because that is all it is. Wishful wonderings of nosy busybodies."

Jacqueline chortled at her friend's denial. "And here I thought you disliked the marquess. However, now I see the attraction for what it is." She turned to Gemma. "It is like that novel we read where the characters hold a troubled relationship with one another until they succumb to their attraction."

Gemma sighed. "Yes, and then they fall in love with one another. I loved that story."

Eden scoffed. "You two are as delusional as my sisters. Now, if you do not mind, I must complete my mission."

Eden started for the door. She refused to touch on this subject even with her closest of friends. However, Gemma and Jacqueline wouldn't let her leave until they made a few adjustments to her appearance. Gemma tugged her bodice back down to display her wares, while Jaqueline pulled her hair back over her shoulders except for a single lock that she draped across her breasts. With shrewd perusals, they nodded in acceptance. Then they stepped to the side for her to pass.

Once she reached the door, Jacqueline dropped a taunt that would linger with Eden for the entire evening. "'Tis not selfish to steal a memory of passion for yourself."

Falcone mingled with the guests, nursing a drink in his hand. The act of depravity began earlier than usual. Usually, the guests waited until they hid their identities behind their masks. Most were peers of the realm and believed they were clever with their disguises where no one recognized them. But everyone knew who walked amongst them and kept their secrets, until they needed the leverage for their own benefit.

Like most gentlemen, he wore a thin mask covering only his eyes. The ladies wore the more elaborate masks decorated with sequins and feathers. They teased a man to discover who they were. His gaze searched the creative masks for his partner for the evening, but none of them were her. He relaxed. Worth must have regained his senses and kept Eden away from this hellish temptation of sin.

He lifted the glass to his mouth. Falcone felt the need to indulge. Why fight against what he must present? If he were to act the reprobate returning to partake in sin this evening, then why shouldn't he enjoy himself while doing so? He drained the glass and signaled the servant for another one.

A girl wearing a fairy costume made of silk and tulle that barely covered her flesh brought him another glass filled with whiskey. He threw the drink back in one gulp as the feathers covering her nipples drew his attention. Maybe if he got drunk enough, the persistent notion of his unfaithfulness to Eden would disappear.

He flicked the feather away to see her nipple tightening. His host this evening had a very clever bride to dress his servants so wickedly. "What might your pleasure be this evening?"

"That is my question for you." She pressed her breast into his hand.

"For starters, I require another refill." His thumb flicked back and forth across her nipple, a sense of his arousal awakening. He held up his other hand with the glass, signaling for her to follow his order.

She took the glass and swished her hips as she sauntered away, glancing over her shoulder to make sure he watched. How could he not? Her buttocks teased him by peeking out from under the sheer gown with each step she took. Mmm. Yes. He would indulge this evening, and the fairy would be his first course. He lost her in the crowd, but he didn't worry because she would return. Her gaze had flashed with her interest when he teased her flesh.

A prickling sense of awareness traveled along his back, and when he shifted his gaze, he saw the very thorn pricking his integrity. No mask could disguise her from him. His body recognized her before his eyes came upon her. The fiery vixen who haunted his every thought pierced him with her gaze. It wasn't a gaze of pleasure, but one filled with fury. And if he wasn't mistaken, a dash of shock mixed with disappointment and hurt. All stirred together, scorching him on the spot.

Eden watched Lord Falcone toy with the servant delivering his drink. She didn't understand why a wave of longing coursed through her body when he held the girl's breast. When his head dipped to whisper in the girl's ear, her curiosity cried out in disappointment at not hearing what he said. Eden wasn't naïve not to realize he propositioned the girl when the servant scampered away to do his bidding. The fairy nymph swayed her body, keeping Falcone's interest firmly attached to her.

She fought against the ache piercing her heart, attempting to deny how his behavior bothered her. Why should she care if he whet his appetite with another? She held no affection for him and only required him to fulfill the same desires the other girl wished for with her provocative clothing and attention. It was then Eden remembered her gown was just as provocative and she was a guest at a party meant for sin. Falcone wasn't the only gentleman who could fulfill her requirements in indulging in the pleasures of the flesh.

Eden dropped the hold of her gaze fastened on Falcone and let it drift across the room. There were many gentlemen who might spark her interest. Who cared if Falcone was the only one who filled out a suit splendidly? She wasn't blind not to see the attention she drew from other gentlemen. Perhaps if she found a different gentleman to ease the ache consuming her, she would forget the emotions Falcone ignited in her.

Her gaze landed on a group of gentlemen who made it obvious they focused their attention on her. Perhaps one of them would do. She grabbed a flute of champagne from a tray and took a gulp to calm her nerves. While she wanted to make her own choice, she must wait. This party did not differ from the balls she attended. The thrill of pursuing a lady excited a man because of the victory he claimed when he won her. So she played the game and smiled coyly at them before wandering into the crowd. Eden made her move. Now she only needed to wait for one of them to make theirs. If she was correct, they would make a contest out of it to win her affection.

Drawing his hands into fists at his side, Falcone scowled at the coy smile Eden flashed the bastards standing in the corner. What game did she play? Did she not understand the smile she flashed them would send them after her in pursuit? He stalked after her, the fairy servant forgotten. Eden had overtaken his interest and wiped any thoughts of another from his mind. His flirtation earlier was but a vague memory of boredom he would never remember.

He followed her as she flittered in between the guests. Curious whispers wondered about her identity, followed by the crude comments about how they would seek their pleasures between her thighs. Falcone wanted to thrash every single one of them, but he couldn't afford to lose sight of Eden. If she disappeared, he would be powerless to save her against the lust-induced scoundrels who tarnished her with their very presence alone.

However, he was no better. He stared at the sway of her hips and imagined his hands digging into them as he plowed in and out of her. When her long legs flashed at him, he growled at the picture of them wrapped around his shoulders as he tasted her sweet cunny. She was a magnificent sight in the sinful dress she wore. What in the hell was Worth thinking to allow his unwed sister to flaunt herself among the reprobates of society?

Falcone reached her before she slipped away from him and drew her behind the columns. When she turned, ready to set down whoever grasped her, he groaned at the display of her breasts swelling out of her gown. Her nipples pressed above the trim, and his cock swelled at the delicious temptation. He licked his lips, eager to savor the sweet berries. His lecture on her earlier behavior was forgotten as her breasts heaved with what he could only guess was irritation over his rough handling.

Eden wasn't a fool to miss that Falcone had followed her. The mirrors she passed showed his reflection within inches of her. Eden had prepared herself for the confrontation when he grasped her and hid them behind the columns. However, she was unprepared for how he would react to her dress. His eyes clouded with passion, and he licked his lips as if he wanted to devour her. Her gaze lowered, and she noticed how his desire pressed against his trousers, on full display for her to see. However, from what she had witnessed earlier, it took little to draw Lord Falcone's interest. He was like every other gentleman here. Filled with lust and would lie between any willing lady's thighs to slake his desires. Well, he would never find pleasure between hers. He had spoiled her interest in him when he touched another. His betrayal pierced her heart in a way she didn't understand and refused to question.

"Should you have left your spot? However will the fairy find you?" Eden laced her comment with sarcasm.

Falcone heard the jealous tone in Eden's voice and realized he had made a grave error with his actions. He pressed her against the column, not saying a word but making her aware of how much she had captured his attention with her beauty. His fingers trailed along her neck, following the path of the necklace. They dipped between her breasts and found the pendant hiding. He drew the jewel out and brushed it across her nipples. His cock throbbed, begging for attention as her buds hardened, pressing against her gown. His fingers twitched to pinch them, but he resisted his desire.

The sound of Eden's soft whimpers showed she held the same desire as him.

"The only spot I wish to occupy is next to you." He bent his head to whisper in her ear. "And a vixen wearing a sinful creation overshadows a mere fairy."

Eden's knees almost gave out at his whispered declaration until she remembered his interest in the wood nymph. She stepped out of his grasp and tried to walk away. But Falcone refused to allow her to escape. He wrapped his arms around her waist and dragged her against his body. Her eyes drifted closed, fighting the passion binding her to him. He pressed against her, sending waves of lust coursing throughout her body. His cock nudged her buttocks, showing her how much he wanted her. But did he desire her or would any willing body do?

His warmth surrounded her, wrapping her in its safe embrace. How she considered the treacherous man safe, Eden held no clue. Her body betrayed her whenever he was near, and for that reason alone, she must resist him. Her plans to seduce him was a colossal mistake on her part. Indulging in sinful pleasures with Falcone would only lead to her heart falling for the devil himself.

Eden shoved at Falcone. "I believe your interest changes to whichever skirt is passing you by. Do not flatter me with your glossy words."

He trailed a finger along her cheek, noticing how her body trembled against him. "I disagree. Your body reveals a different story."

Before Eden uttered a protest, Falcone covered her mouth with his in a forceful kiss to quiet her. He maneuvered his body to hide her from any curious eyes. It was dark enough that no one saw who captured his attention. As much as she protested against her attraction to him, her lips were quick to soften under his.

Hell! He wanted to lose himself in her kisses. They were the opposite of what poured out of her snarling mouth. Soft. Gentle. Full of curiosity. What he wouldn't give to explore their desire, but unfortunately he must wait. He must stay on guard at how he manipulated them at this party and not expose their vulnerabilities. Too many people observed their behavior and waited to strike if they slipped out of character.

"Who are you looking for?"

"The blond beauty who flashed us a come-hither smile. Who else?"

Voices reached Eden through the dizziness of Falcone's kisses. They weren't discussing her, were they? Her eyes flashed open, and she thrashed her head to the side to halt their kiss. Falcone grabbed her chin back to him and gave a slight shake of his head to stay silent. She nodded.

The gentleman had a slimy voice. "Maybe I've already claimed her for my conquest this evening."

"I do not see her on your arm. So she is fair game," the man with the squeaky voice declared.

"As long as Falcone doesn't get near her. Ever since the bastard returned, every female falls at his feet," Slimy said.

"The fairy snared his attention."

Slimy laughed. "That piece will keep him occupied for the evening."

Squeaky joined in, laughing. "A proper punishment for the marquess. As for the blond beauty, perhaps you would be open to sharing her this evening."

Eden's eyes widened. She opened her mouth to protest when Falcone's finger pressed against it.

"Stay silent," he whispered.

"A promising suggestion. Perhaps we should resume our search so we can properly enjoy this party," Slimy agreed.

A shudder racked Eden at the possibility of these men finding her. She didn't have the skills to avoid their propositions. Perhaps Falcone stood correct on not having her attend this party. She had never imagined such depravity took place.

Falcone wrapped her in his embrace, offering her comfort. Or at least she fooled herself to believe that was what he offered. "I will never allow another man to touch you," Falcone swore in her ear.

She closed her eyes, leaning into him. She knew he only meant to reassure her of their present situation, but a small part of her wished his statement was true.

"Let me check behind these columns, then we can move on," Slimy said.

Once again, Falcone kissed Eden, and she returned the kiss with desperation. Only she didn't know if it was from fear of the gentlemen finding her or her desperate need to have Falcone's lips tempting her toward a passion out of control. Either way, she clung to him and met him kiss for kiss. Her hands dove into his hair, pulling his head closer.

Falcone's control at maintaining their secrecy slipped away at Eden's response. She responded with a passion that made him forget why he must keep her identity a secret. He heard a noise from behind them and shielded Eden from the danger lurking after her.

"Did you find her?" Squeaky asked.

"No. But I saw Falcone with another piece of fluff. Lucky for us, it wasn't the blond beauty. We must find her before he charms her."

Their voices drifted away, but Eden never ended the kiss. Soon her fear subsided with each gentle pull of Falcone's lips against hers. And still she continued kissing him. So lost in the spell surrounding them, she forgot what had prompted Falcone to kiss her. She only wished for Falcone to touch her beyond holding her in his embrace.

However, Falcone had other ideas. He pulled away from the kiss, grabbed her arm, and led her in the opposite direction of where the gentlemen searched. They immersed themselves deeper in the crowd before Falcone swept Eden into a dance. A dance never shared in the ballroom floors of London. But one where their bodies molded together in an endless dance of seduction.

The dance made Eden aware of her desire for Falcone. It went above and beyond anything she had felt before. Each twist and turn sent her spiraling further out of control with a desperation only Falcone could appease. She didn't wonder if Falcone felt the same. Not with the way his hands roamed over her body as he guided her along in the steps. Each caress held a deeper intimacy. His hardness pressed against her stomach, giving Eden proof of his need for her.

"I want to spread you out on my bed and worship every inch of your luscious body with soft kisses and gentle caresses before I take you with a need so powerful I cannot control myself. Where you will claw at my back with your own desperation. Where your screams will rock the walls. Where your heels will dig into my back as you meet me thrust for thrust. Where I will forge an ache in your soul that no other man can appease." Falcone's voice deepened with each request.

His statement left Eden a quivering mess. The rational side of her demanded for her to run far away, while the side of her that craved danger begged Eden to follow Falcone wherever he led her.

Falcone swung her out from him in a twirl before bringing her back against him. "Just so that we are clear. My declaration was not a request but a promise, so you are not mistaken about my intentions."

He sealed it off with a searing kiss, leaving Eden in no doubt about how their evening would end.

Chapter Six

A S QUICKLY AS FALCONE drew her in a seductive dance, he and Eden were off again, traversing down a darkened hallway, only this time they trailed along with his arm wrapped around her waist, keeping her close to his side.

In the first room they passed, a couple was wrapped in an intimate embrace, sharing kisses. Then each room they passed held people in various positions of debauchery. The deeper they traveled, the more decadent they grew. Falcone kept striding faster, but Eden craned her neck to catch a glimpse. Along the way, other people stood outside the rooms, watching. A crowd of voyeurs staring into the library blocked their path when they reached the end of the hallway.

As Falcone pushed their way through, his arm got disengaged from around her. Eden's curiosity urged her to take a peek before finding Falcone again. She inched her way forward, unprepared for what she would find. She thought she would discover another couple embraced, sharing a few kisses. But the sight she met wiped away any naïve thoughts she had about the party she attended.

A variety of couples was spread across the furniture in stages of undress, taking part in lustful relations, each act more sinful than the next. Her gaze landed on a lady with her head nestled on a gentleman's lap while another man pleasured her from behind. Eden averted her gaze but landed on a lady lying on a divan with her skirts pushed above her waist with a man's head between her thighs. The lady tugged at the man's hair, clasping his head in place. It didn't shock Eden as much as the another man forcing his cock into the lady's mouth at a maddening pace. However, the lady didn't fight the attack but held onto the man's buttocks with her other hand.

A warmth overcame Eden she didn't understand. Her gaze darted around, watching the two scenes. The other couples didn't draw her attention or else she couldn't handle taking in any more of the depravity. Their moans played a symphony from their pleasures.

Falcone had lost Eden. His gaze searched the voyeurs and found her near the front of the crowd. He shoved his way through to her and discovered her entranced by the scene. A blush spread across her body, and her tongue kept darting out to wet her lips. His gaze lowered to her nipples, which had pebbled into tight little buds, and her chest rose and fell with her quickened breaths. If he slid his hand up the slit in her dress and sank it into her cunny, would she be as wet as he thought she was? And how would she taste?

He observed her as her eyes darted back and forth between two different scenes, her breathing growing more agitated. Eden's hand rose and wrapped around her necklace, dipping the stone up and down between the valley of her breasts. She didn't even realize how her actions stroked his desire to claim her. Hell, his need to spend himself while watching her getting aroused by others made its demands. He fought the need to pull out his cock and stroke himself until he branded her with his mark. And no one would care. Because that was how depraved everyone surrounding them was.

But he refused to ruin Eden in the sinful atmosphere, no matter how much he wanted to stroke her pussy and have her come on his fingers while the scene before them captured her attention. He wouldn't subject her to the depravity he kept tampered, no matter how tempting of a sight she was before him now.

To end the madness pulling him under, he drew her away slowly so as not to startle her. Once he separated them from the crowd, he pushed Eden up against the wall until her gaze once again focused on him.

Falcone stared as her sapphire eyes lit up, only to darken again when she stared at his lips. He must continue resisting her and stay focused on their agenda. He would satisfy her needs once they finished setting their trap. "Come, we have a job to finish."

Falcone didn't give Eden a chance to reply. Her reaction to the scene mortified her, and his silence was a welcome relief. She never imagined those acts were possible. Oh, she had a slight clue about the passion a couple might share. She had read her share of books and witnessed enough passionate exchanges at entertainments to draw her own conclusions, but she never realized multiple people indulged in the act of sex together. What she had just witnessed wasn't lovemaking, but the pure lust of sex.

Eden stayed close to Falcone and never strayed from him again. She didn't know if she could handle any other intimate displays. Falcone kept her close as he exchanged pleasantries with the gentlemen and flirted with the ladies. Eden paid little attention to any of his exchanges. The flirtation toward the other ladies was only the smooth words of a charmer to distract them from his agenda. She recognized the difference between these ladies and how he had propositioned the fairy.

He wanted the fairy in his bed, while these ladies served a purpose to gain information.

Eden's silence unsettled Falcone. She didn't resist his possessive hold but leaned into it during his conversations. Her thoughts appeared lost. With what? He wished to know. Was she in shock at what she had witnessed? Or what he had promised her? Either way, he regretted letting Worth and Ralston talk him into this. They never should have subjected Eden to the events of the evening.

He finished his discussion and led Eden over to the alcove. He was curious to learn what occupied her thoughts, to make sense of why she never engaged with him since the scene from the library.

"Eden?" He brushed a lock of hair away from her face.

Her eyes drifted up toward his. "Mmm."

His need to touch her prompted him to rub his hands up and down her arms. "Talk to me. Say something that annoys me. Anything but your silence."

"If I do, will you kiss me again?" Eden whispered.

Falcone groaned. Her question wasn't what he expected. He had no intention of their evening ending on honorable terms. No, he would take her to his home and seduce her until she screamed his name in pleasure. He kept telling himself seducing Eden was part of his revenge, but it was a lie. He had wanted Eden Worthington since the day he met her and she attempted to tear his honorable intentions to shreds. Each snarl she delivered his way only intensified his need. Even now, she brought him to his knees with her simple question. However, he saw it for what it truly was. It wasn't a simple question, but an invitation to her heart. Did he covet her heart, and if so, why?

Instead of replying to her question with charming words, he pressed his lips against hers in an act of seduction. Falcone never acted with honorable intentions, so why should he now?

Eden sighed into his gentle kiss. She had waited for his kiss since he tore her away from the scene in the library. She thirsted for the heady intoxication only his kisses would offer her. Her body sparked to life again. However, it longed for the passion he had described to her.

"I didn't even say anything," Eden murmured between their kisses.

Falcone trailed a path of kisses along her neck. "God, woman, you never have to utter a word for me to desire to claim your lips under mine."

"Oh." Eden gasped, not only from his declaration but also from how he bit her neck. "Perhaps we should leave now."

"Soon," he muttered, his lips trailing lower.

"Mmm." Eden didn't argue because he distracted her by searing a path of fire across her chest. His tongue dipped between her breasts, licking at her flesh. When his tongue traced over the curve of her partially revealed nipple, an ache pierced her core. Her need whimpered out from between her lips, and Falcone pinched her nipple between his fingers, changing her whimper to a deep-throated moan.

Falcone captured her moan in another kiss. He tasted her need with each lick of his tongue. A need that only intensified his own.

"Lord Falcone," a voice whispered in the distance.

At least he thought it was a whisper. However, the source of the voice pressed against his back and slid her hand along the front of his trousers. He spun around and grabbed her hand before she reached for the source of her interest. It would appear he needed to teach the whore a lesson at touching him without his permission. He tightened his grip harder, sending his message loud and clear without words. Eden was the only woman ever allowed to touch his cock. He wouldn't have this slut tarnish his heightened emotions for the lady behind him by touching him like she had permission to do so.

"Melody. Have you fulfilled my request?"

Melody nodded, and he released his hold. But she didn't get his message and pressed against him again, stroking her hands along his chest. To make matters worse, Eden had stepped to his side and was watching their exchange. Her mood evaporated with the glare she directed his way.

"If you will excuse me, it appears as if I am no longer needed," Eden snarled.

Falcone grabbed her before she stalked away. He rubbed her wrist in a gentle motion, trying to calm her temper. She misunderstood his exchange with Melody, but he must learn if certain people believed in his ruse to return to his old lifestyle.

"No need to excuse yourself, luv. I do not mind sharing Lord Falcone." Melody reached out to touch Eden, but Falcone swiped her hand out of the way before she soiled Eden with her touch.

Eden arched her eyebrows as only a lady of the aristocracy could. "I, however, do."

Falcone needed to send Melody on her way before he lost what he shared with Eden. "What have you learned?"

"There has been much laughter about how you have fallen from grace, and they are taking bets on when you will cross over to Lady L's side. I even overheard Lady L's interest in why you visit your old haunts. I slipped the information you gave me into one of her guard's ears while he fucked me. Just the way you asked me to. Before long, Lady L should hear of your downfall," Melody explained.

"Excellent. You did well." Falcone pushed her away. "Now run along."

"When is our next lesson?" Melody asked, drawing her bodice to the side to reveal her breast. She stroked her finger along the nipple.

"When you have more information I need." Falcone waved his hand for her to leave.

Melody stared at Eden as she answered him. "I cannot wait. Maybe she can join us, and I will teach her how to please you."

Before Falcone silenced Melody's taunts, Eden stalked away. However, unknown to her, she headed toward the gentlemen who sought her company. He had kept her away from their attention, but soon she would be within their grasp. Falcone rushed after her, with Melody's disturbing laughter echoing behind him. She was an issue he would address later. Since he found success with the evening, he needed to remove Eden from the sin she never should have seen.

He reached for her as she turned back. He looked beyond her and saw the reason for her change in direction. The two gentlemen who searched for Eden had caught sight of her and started toward her. Her eyes pleaded with him to make their escape. Falcone pulled Eden in front of him and guided her toward the foyer. However, before they slipped away, their host for the evening stopped them.

"You are not leaving so soon, are you, Falcone? The evening is still young, with so many delights still to be enjoyed," Lord Chesterton stated, swaying on his feet.

"The lady and I will continue our delights in the privacy of my home." Falcone kissed Eden's neck to display his intentions.

"Nonsense," Chesterton slurred. "Your usual bedchamber awaits your pleasure. I heard of your return and have prepared it with all your usual needs."

"I prefer to introduce the lady to my particular enjoyments in my own bed, where I can entice her to stay on for a few days afterwards," Falcone explained.

Eden listened to Falcone explain his reason for their departure. However, Chesterton insisted they stay. She glanced over her shoulder to see the gentlemen had followed them. Their lewd glances made Eden uncomfortable, and she wished Falcone would hurry this conversation along so they could escape. She had stepped into unchartered territory this evening and wished only for the comfort of her home.

"You have yet to meet my bride. I've told her all about you, and she pleaded for an introduction. Here she comes now. Amuse me a while longer, Falcone, then you can indulge in the delights of this creature. I can understand the urgency to get her alone since her packaging is quite tempting." Chesterton leered at Eden. "I wonder if she tastes as delicious as she looks. I wouldn't mind a nibble of my own. She looks sweet, but I suspect her flavor is intoxicating. Perhaps after you savored her delights, I can try a sample."

"Like hell," Falcone growled.

The ferocity in Falcone's tone took Chesterton by surprise. However, the depraved gentleman only smiled wickedly when Falcone revealed his feelings for Eden. Falcone cursed himself for displaying his weakness. Their need to leave was stronger now than ever.

"Ah, she must be unique. Usually you do not mind sharing. Oh well, I am a patient man and can wait until you tire of her. For now, allow me to introduce you to my lovely bride."

Falcone pasted on a smile and fought to keep it as the fairy stood on her tiptoes to kiss Chesterton. He glanced at Eden and would've laughed at her shocked expression if he didn't hold the same reaction.

"Darling, here is your chance to meet the notorious Lord Falcone." Chesterton smiled adoringly at his bride.

The fairy stroked her hand inside her husband's shirt and smiled seductively at Falcone. "Oh, the lord and I have already met. But he disappeared before we became better acquainted."

"Then perhaps you can convince him and his lovely paramour to enjoy our party a bit longer."

She pouted at Falcone. "You cannot leave yet. I hear it is bad form for a guest to leave before he has enjoyed the host's hospitality. I know in my country it is."

Falcone hadn't recognized the fairy's French accent until now. That alerted him to the connection she might hold with Lady Langdale, the very lady who stood nearby.

As much as he hated to subject Eden to the crude behavior, he must play the part of a degenerate reprobate to convince everyone of his downfall. His hand closed over Eden's breast, molding it in his hand while he bent his head and nuzzled her neck.

"Play along," he hissed.

It was vital that Eden follow his lead. If not, then she risked exposure and it would ruin their entire operation. When she threw her head back and moaned, he knew she had received his message and agreed to follow his lead.

"You may have a point, Lord Chesterton. I do not believe we will make it to my residence before my cock finds the satisfaction it needs. My urge to plow between her thighs is making its own demand." He turned Eden toward the stairs. "My old bedchamber, you say?"

"Yes. For a more sinful indulgence, I offer my wife in gratitude for accepting our generous offer."

Falcone paused, unsure how to respond. He didn't want to draw attention by refusing his host's gift, but he forbade another soul anywhere near them.

"Oui. I would enjoy teaching your lady in the art of lovemaking. Perhaps show her how to suck your cock until you beg for release." The fairy stepped forward and palmed his cock. His cock had remained hard since Eden appeared wearing a creation molded to her body like sin itself.

He didn't need to worry about how to handle the situation because Eden staked her possession. She tugged the fairy's wrist away before stepping in front of him. "This lady has no need for anyone to teach her how to please the marquess. She is perfectly capable of drawing out his pleas while she sucks his cock on her own. You see, her appetite is plentiful and will only find fulfillment with him alone. While we thank you for your generous offer, Lord Chesterton, we must decline this evening." She turned around and stared into Falcone's eyes. "Perhaps another evening we might be more amenable to other *indulgences.*"

Lord Chesterton laughed. "Ahh, now I see the allure, Falcone. She is a fiery vixen you will never tame. However, I believe you will enjoy trying. Come, my dear, we have other guests to attend."

"Yes, perhaps another time, mademoiselle," the fairy replied as her husband drew her away.

Falcone held no idea what to make of Eden's stare. The sapphires flashed the many sparks of her emotions, never wavering once. He wanted to decipher each spark and delve into what they meant, but the sense of danger lurking behind him prompted him to break their spell. He looked around and noticed the party continued. However, he knew differently.

"Shall we, Lord Falcone?" Eden's husky whisper interrupted his search for danger.

He had no choice but to lead her to the sin that awaited them. "This way, my lady."

He only hoped he held the strength not to indulge.

Chapter Seven

F ALCONE TOOK EDEN'S HAND, leading her up the stairs and along the hallway lit with candles in scones. All the doors were closed, but they didn't remain empty. Lord Chesterton reserved them for the lords and ladies who didn't wish for an audience and required the privacy to indulge in their vices of pleasure. The bedchamber reserved for him was at the end of the hallway. The room spanned the length of the hallway, converting two bedchambers into one designed for whatever the master of the domain desired.

He cringed when he escorted Eden inside. His past had left its tarnished reputation painted across every object decorating the chamber. He closed the door and tore off his mask. With his back to Eden, he slid the locks into place. No one could access the bedchamber, nor would they dare if they valued their life.

Falcone turned and found Eden reclining on the divan. Her head rested on her arm, and the mask dangled from her fingers. Her eyes followed him as he strode across the room and poured himself a drink. After throwing back the shot, he poured himself another, filled to the rim. He moved back to settle into a chair close to Eden and stretched out his legs. With a weary sigh, he worked on draining the glass.

Falcone glanced at Eden and found her gaze stayed focused on him. He owed her an explanation, but he didn't know where to start. He took another drink for courage. "I apologize. I hoped we would make our escape without drawing the host's notice. If we wait until the early hours, we can leave once everyone has passed out from their drunken revelry."

Eden twirled the ribbons on the mask, causing it to spin around. The movement matched the emotions twisting inside her. One moment she wanted to revel in the mastery of Falcone's seduction, then the next she wanted to rant at him about the hussies who attempted their seduction on him. She knew she paled in comparison because of her inexperience.

She had wondered about Falcone's past. However, after this evening, she held a clear picture of his debaucherous lifestyle. Her only question was if he missed the throes of decadence. After the many sights she had witnessed, she understood how one was unable to release the bonds that kept them indulging in the decadent sin.

"Does it really matter?" Eden asked.

Falcone frowned, unsure what her question meant. "Yes. Your safety matters."

Eden let the mask slip from her fingers and watched it drift to the floor. She raised her eyes to Falcone. "And my virtue?"

Once again, Eden's husky question left him speechless. He cleared his throat and attempted a retort, but nothing came forth. He threw back the rest of the drink and tried again. "Your virtue is the most important matter of all."

"Is it?"

"Yes."

"Of course it is. It was the very matter of your seduction the entire evening, was it not?" Eden slid her leg across her other one, opening the slit on her dress to expose herself to Falcone.

Falcone gripped the glass, wishing he had more to drink. While he desired to seduce Eden, he didn't want to ruin her in the very room of his downfall. "My seduction? You are mistaken, Lady Eden. I only played a part, just as I assumed you were."

He lied. Another fault she could lay blame at his feet, but one he did to protect her. So for that, Eden would allow him the slight flaw. The gentleman held many flaws. Most of them were frustrating, but a few struck her interest to the reason he held them.

Downstairs, her temper had been ignited by yet another lady overlooking her presence at his side and propositioning him. However, she had noted the panic in his gaze when he realized the fairy was Lord Chesterton's bride. Yet, when each woman propositioned him, Falcone had shown no sign of interest. But his disinterest never swayed them; it only encouraged them to keep trying. However, he had stayed firm with his dismissal of them, much different from how he treated her this evening.

While she didn't throw herself at Falcone, she still showed her interest in how she responded to his seduction. Each exchange heightened their desire. Lord Falcone didn't fool her for a minute with his denial. He wanted her. Desperately, if she wasn't mistaken. The reason for his resistance puzzled her.

She glanced around the room. It spoke of seduction, from the silken bedsheets to the candles shining in a façade of romance. Rose petals trailed a path to the bed and toward a set of pillows near the fireplace. A tub rested near the windows with flowers circling the pedestals. No romance would occur in this bedchamber, only the pure desperation of lost souls claiming peace for a brief space of time.

Eden rose and walked over to Falcone, enjoying how unsteady she made him. She slid the glass out of his grasp to refill his drink. She carried it back to him and slipped between his splayed legs, taking a sip. The whiskey burned a path of fire down her throat and settled in her stomach, where it flared out into a welcoming warmth. She placed the glass back in his hand before she lowered herself to the floor between his sprawled-out legs.

Eden trailed her hands up his legs, spreading her fingers across his muscular thighs. "Playing a part, you say?" Her fingers teased higher.

What in the hell did the vixen play at? Was this her idea of revenge for his crass treatment of her in front of Lord Chesterton?

Her fingers brushed across his cock. Its hardness showed proof of how he lied to her. If she didn't rise, she would soon learn a lesson on why she shouldn't tease a man in this sense. However, she remained, her nimble fingers unbuttoning the placket on his trouser.

He covered her hand with his own. "Do not start what you do not intend to finish."

Eden ignored Falcone's warning and pushed his hand away, resuming her task. "Oh, but I intend to finish, Lord Falcone."

Falcone gripped her fingers. "Stop this nonsense, Eden. You have made your point. Now rise and go sit on the divan like a proper girl and wait until we can leave."

Eden pouted up at him. "Perhaps I wish to be naughty."

Eden didn't know what prompted her to speak so scandalously, nor did she care. Her body ached for the touch of Falcone. He had built the passion surrounding them to a fever pitch, leaving Eden wanting him to satisfy her every need. She refused to allow him to change his mind about his seduction. If he would no longer continue, then she would.

Her ruby-red lips glistened in the candlelight, making him yearn for them to slide down his cock and suck him dry. His view as he gazed down at her gave him a glimpse of the bosom that had teased him all evening. The flickering of the light displayed the sheerness of her gown and showed him lush berries, beckoning him to savor them. He sat ogling her instead of stopping her. He lost his ability to resist her when she opened the placket of his trousers and drew out his cock. Perhaps he was more depraved than he thought to allow Eden to service him when she was a complete innocent.

Eden was aware of how wanton she was by seducing Falcone. But she gave him no choice to act the honorable gentleman when he had teased her with his seduction all evening. She wanted to make him forget every woman who had ever propositioned him and leave her mark on him so he'd never forget her.

Her hand wrapped around his hardness and slid it up and down. A deep growl came from him, and she glanced up, stopping her movement, afraid she had caused him harm. Falcone had thrown his head back with his eyes closed. When she stopped, his eyelids had raised but a sliver, and his look pleaded for her to continue. She dipped her head and smiled at her victory.

His cock throbbed, pulsing its own beat of need. The velvety smoothness glided like a dream in her hand. Her thumb brushed across the wet dew seeping out of the tip of his cock, and she spread it out along the length of him. Her action drew out another throaty groan from Falcone. Eden's tongue brushed across the tip, tasting the slickness.

"God have mercy on me," Falcone prayed, but he never stopped her sweet torture.

Falcone hovered between heaven and hell. Allowing Eden to pleasure him was the most exquisite act he had ever enjoyed, one that would deliver him straight to the devil for not refusing her. But what man alive would ever stop a vixen this glorious from wrapping her ruby-red lips around their cock?

None. Even a saint would sing his praises to God for enjoying such an act.

Eden held no clue what she was supposed to do, but she let her instincts guide her in offering Falcone pleasure. With each of his groans, she smiled and tried something different to draw out more. She remembered the ladies she had watched in the library and how they pleasured the gentlemen they were with. So, she wrapped her lips around his cock and lowered her mouth, drawing him deep within. This brought out a rumble of a groan that shook his body.

Eden pulled him out and stroked him as she caught her breath. She looked up coyly from her lashes and caught him staring at her with such an intensity that it stole her breath away.

Falcone tried to steady his breathing, but she stole the very air surrounding him. Not only the air, but every sane part of him. He would never be the same again. He wasn't blind to the coy glances she gave him. She wanted him at her mercy, begging for salvation. If he didn't show his indifference soon, she would see the hold she had over him and relentlessly strive to keep him under her control.

He lifted the glass and took a sip, savoring the fiery heat. He didn't need it to warm his soul. No, Eden managed that all on her own. He drank to give himself courage not to succumb to the lady's charms. But as he drank one sip after another, Falcone realized he was already a doomed man. He had fallen for her charms long before he even realized it.

Eden wanted to wipe the smirk from Falcone's lips as he nonchalantly drank the whiskey. His indifference was false. If not, his breathing would have stayed steady instead of erratic. And his fingers wouldn't clutch the glass as if his life depended on it. No. Lord Falcone was anything but calm, and she would prove it.

Her mouth lowered over his cock, her tongue dragging along his length as she drew him in deeper. This time, she opened her mouth to breathe in little bursts of air as she slid him in and out. Her tongue teased him, showing him no mercy. The sound of glass breaking and whiskey splashing against her legs didn't stop her torment. It only increased as he speared his hands into her hair and guided her along.

With each pull of her lips on his cock, Falcone lost what remained of his control. His hands tightened in her locks of hair as she sent him spiraling over the pinnacle of pleasure. Her tongue sent licks of fire to his core. He roared his pleasure when she took him over the edge.

Falcone's roar echoed around them, rocking the very foundation Eden thought she controlled. But she realized she was as powerless as he was to their passion. When she raised her head and wiped her thumb across her lips, he let out another roar that made her tremble. Her teasing had far surpassed anything she might ever imagine. He stood up, towering above her as if he were her king and she a lowly servant whose only position was to serve him. But when he lifted her in his arms and carried her to the bed, she realized she wasn't the servant but his queen instead.

Falcone never spoke a word. The lady turned him into a speechless fool. A fool who had believed he held no feelings for her. That she was a means for revenge was another lie he had spoken. This woman undid him like no other.

He stripped the gown from her body and stared at the vixen spread out amongst the silken sheets like the goddess she was. No profound declaration could be made to describe her beauty. Only gentle caresses and soft kisses would do to show the effect she held over his senses.

He started with her lips and then made his way to her breasts. The ruby lay between her globes as a warning to stop. He still had time to act like a gentleman and protect her innocence. But the jewel was also a symbol of the fiery passion they ignited whenever they were near one another. Since he wasn't a gentleman, he saw no need to pretend otherwise. Especially when he had a vixen willingly spread before him to feast upon.

With a wicked smile, Falcone lowered his head and drew her nipple between his lips. Eden whimpered at the exquisite torture and drew her hand through his locks.

She moaned. "Oh, Falcone."

He raised his head. "Victor," he growled.

"Victor."

He rewarded her by sucking harder on the pebbled bud. Her fingers glided through his hair, and he increased the pressure of his lips. His other hand cupped the other breast and pinched the nipple. She responded freely, but it made him impatient to hear her screams. He lowered his hand to dip into her curls and sank into her wetness. God. She was a vixen indeed.

Victor slid along her body, spreading kisses over every silken inch of her. When he reached her thighs, he made his need known by his command. "Open your thighs, Eden, I want a taste of your sweet cunny. It is only fair I repay you in kind."

Eden needed no other encouragement to obey him. She was at his mercy. As long as he never stopped, she'd follow his every command. Victor branded her with each kiss and caress. Her legs spread open, and she welcomed him to pleasure her. However, as much as she ached for him to kiss her, she was unprepared for the onslaught of mercy he stole from her with each lick of his tongue.

Victor didn't see it as an act of revenge as he made Eden tremble underneath his mouth, but an act of worship. As he savored each drop of her sweetness on his tongue, he realized the creation of Eden was for him alone. He slid a finger inside her, gliding it in and out as his tongue dipped along her folds. Another finger slid inside, and her pussy tightened around them, drawing them in deeper. Eden's whimpers grew louder, and her body moved restlessly, seeking its release.

He pressed his thumb against her clit and held still. "Easy, love. All in due time," Victor whispered before flicking the nub back and forth.

Eden tried to follow Victor's advice, but her body made other demands. "Falcone, please spare me," Eden begged.

He slid two fingers in deeper while his tongue soothed her soft nub. "Now why should I show mercy when you cannot even address me properly between the bedsheets?"

He teased her by blowing soft breaths against her core. Eden thrashed her head back and forth on the pillow as the warm brush of air breathed fire on her.

"Falcone." She didn't even recognize her own voice.

He pulled his fingers out of her pussy and raised his head, waiting for her to moan his God-given name. His fingers sank into her thighs as he fought against his own need. He watched how her need possessed her body, taking over with its own demand. But his demand would take precedence over hers. When she spoke his name, it was only Victor and Eden lost in the paradise they created. But when she called out Falcone, it reminded him too much of the friction between them. And he wanted no friction separating them while they made love. He only wanted the sweet sensation of their love embracing them.

Eden's eyes flashed open, her body protesting at the loss of his touch. Why had he stopped? Her eyes met his, and her heart melted. There were no words to describe how the longing in his gaze affected her.

She moaned. "Victor."

Her simple reply was all that it took for him to resume his sweet torture. The husky sound of her need as she moaned his name turned his drive to send her over the edge, an obsession he would take pleasure from. There were no gentle nips and strokes this time. He unleashed the passion he kept contained and sent her tumbling into the abyss with each bold stroke of his tongue licking and sucking on her succulent juices. Victor prepared Eden's pussy for his cock with each tug of his fingers sliding in and out.

Eden screamed when he sent her tumbling, and he licked up every drop of desire clinging to her pussy, whispering calming words to help soothe her trembling soul. Victor rose above her and slid inside, pushing past the slight barrier, and settled himself as deeply as he could. Eden stiffened for a brief moment before she wrapped her arms around him.

Slowly, he slid out and back in. In and out, he speared inside her deeper, his pace increasing. She drove him wild when her legs rose and pressed against his hips. He clasped onto one of them and angled himself to hit her deep in her core, rotating his hips. Her whimpers and moans fueled his demand to possess her.

Eden arched into Victor, and her nipples hardened at the roughness of his chest. A shot of desire coursed through her. She pressed soft kisses along his neck, but they turned hungrier when he increased the rhythm he set for them. With each pump of his hips against hers, Victor settled in deeper and harder. Her fingernails dug into his back, leaving another mark by scratching him. His hand dipped to tease her clit with soft strokes of his thumb, while his cock gave her no mercy and demanded her release.

Eden's lips branded him while she called out his name and stole the last of his restraint. He plunged inside her, screaming her name as he came apart in her arms. Eden's pussy gripped his cock with her slight tremors as she joined him.

He rolled over and drew her into his arms. He didn't know whose body shook more. Hers or his. Victor only knew that Eden Worthington shook the very foundation he struggled to stand on.

Would she still want him when it crumbled around him?

Chapter Eight

FALCONE STROKED HIS HAND along Eden's hair. His fingers luxuriated in the soft texture. Eden had fallen asleep after they made love, saving him from an awkward conversation. What did one say to the very lady who had made it clear since they met how she didn't hold a high opinion of him? While her behavior offended him, he also found amusement in her snide remarks, taunting her in return. Her dislike of his character never bothered him before. However, now he stood on unstable ground about her opinion of him. Whatever that may be.

His gaze traveled around the room, and he recalled every moment he had spent inside it. The horrors of his past flashed before him. He shut his eyes, trying to block out the scene that haunted him every day. When he opened his eyes, his gaze landed on Eden. Another sight that would haunt his memories. However, her sprawled across him was a memory he would welcome every day.

Eden's warm body lay on top of him, her curves nestled into his roughness. Her face relaxed in sleep with her mouth slightly open, wearing only a trace of the bold lip color. His cock sported the rest. Just reminding himself how her lips sucked him off caused his cock to harden. The vixen had seduced him, and he had been powerless to resist her. His thumb slid over her bottom lip, and Eden mumbled out a moan but remained sleeping.

Her fingers were curled on his chest, and he lifted them to his mouth and pressed a kiss on the knuckle where his ring would sit. He had never wanted to marry. Not because he wished to remain a bachelor or refused to carry on the family line. His reason rested with how he never wished for any lady to endure a marriage spent in apprehension of whether he would return to the hedonism lifestyle he had once craved. This evening only proved how easily he manipulated the lifestyle to fit his needs. Debauchery coursed through his veins as easily as the lies that spilled off his tongue.

However jaded he was, he must offer Eden the respect she deserved. His intention had been to seek revenge with his seduction, but she had struck instead. Now everything he had ever wanted shifted to include Eden. He would act the honorable gentleman, no matter how far removed he was, and offer for her hand in marriage.

He couldn't ask her in the traditional sense by requesting an audience with her older brother Reese Worthington for her hand. Nor could he inform Eden of his intentions. The lady would refuse and insist their time together was a product of a sexually induced evening. She would prattle on about her curiosity and how their actions had resulted because of their attraction to one another. Then she would reassure him by stating she had no inclination to marry him. He must find a creative way to show Eden how unbearable her existence was without him. Then he would make his offer.

For now, he would act as the callous gentleman and proposition her. He smiled as he pictured her reaction. While he had never desired to be bound to another, an eternity with Eden changed everything. He was willing to put aside his doubts to find out. Falcone looked forward to the future.

He slid out from underneath her, pulling the sheet over her body. She was a distraction enough, lying spread out in all her splendid glory. If he continued staring at her beauty, they would never leave. If they didn't return soon, then Eden wouldn't have a choice. She would find herself married to him, regardless of how she felt.

He slipped on his clothes and stepped into the hallway. He signaled to the footman and ordered his carriage to be brought around to the front. Lord Chesterton stepped out of the shadows after the footman scurried away to do his bidding. Falcone scowled at him.

Chesterton held up his hands in peace. "I am sorry, mate. But you had to realize if you left, it would have compromised your assignment. Not to mention you risked revealing Lady Eden's identity."

Falcone advanced on Chesterton and put his arm against his throat. "Never utter her name."

Chesterton nodded. "I apologize," he croaked out.

Falcone dropped his arm but stayed close by. "Then it was a success?"

"Yes. Lady L has requested a meeting to discuss your treason."

"Treason?" Falcone scoffed. "Does she believe she is dealing with a government agency like we are at war? God! She has always been a dramatic bitch."

"Yes. But she holds the power to filch the fortunes of the esteemed peerage."

"Stall her for a couple of days while I discuss this new twist with Worth and Ralston. For now, I must escort my guest for the evening home."

"Be careful. Lady L has men following you," Chesterton warned.

Falcone turned toward the door. "I figured she would, and I planned accordingly." He turned back. "Did you and the fairy marry or is it a ruse?"

Chesterton took on a pinched expression. "Colebourne insisted on it. He said it made it appear more authentic."

Falcone shook his head at the duke's involvement. They were all puppets, and he pulled the strings. He would pull his own strings after he finished working on this case. "I'll be in touch."

Chesterton never replied and disappeared back into the shadows as if their conversation had never happened.

Falcone stepped inside and gathered Eden's clothing before sitting on the bed. He gently shook her. "Eden, love. We must leave."

Eden stretched, and the sheet slipped away, leaving Falcone with a full view of her exquisite beauty. He rubbed his hand along his cock to ease the ache overcoming him as he stared at her bountiful breasts and the berries that begged for him to take a bite. His gaze lowered, and his fingers itched to stroke her awake.

"Mmm," Eden murmured.

His gaze flashed to her face, and when he saw the desire shining in her eyes and her mouth lifting into a vixen's smile, he leapt to his feet. He must not give in to temptation no matter how seductive she looked.

He cleared his throat and moved as far away from the bed as he possibly could. "You need to dress. We must leave before everyone awakens and someone notices you."

Eden didn't know whether to smile at how flustered Falcone acted or frown at his proper demeanor. However, she was aware of the seriousness of their situation. As much as she desired to tempt him under the covers, she must prepare to leave. She couldn't afford to have her reputation tarnished. Nor would she disgrace her family with her selfishness.

She slid the gown back on and drew the stockings up her legs before slipping back into the heels she had worn. She gathered her reticule and glanced out the window to notice they had little time. The sky grew lighter with the rising sun. She hoped Worth hadn't worried over their delay too much.

"You may turn, Falcone. I am decent." Eden smoothed a hand along her skirt.

Falcone turned and frowned. He didn't care for how she addressed him. Had they not moved passed the need for formality once he sank his cock into her cunny? By Eden's expression, she thought differently. He sighed. He would deal with her change of mood after he got her safely into his carriage.

Falcone strode to Eden's side, took off his suit coat, and covered her with it. Any attempt to keep her hidden was better than nothing. It only took one sober peer to recognize anything familiar about her and the gossip would spread. He searched the floor for the piece that would guarantee her safety. The mask was lying near the divan where Eden had dropped it while accusing him of seducing her all evening. He scooped it up, allowing himself a brief smirk at how correct she had been.

With his serious expression back in place, he asked her to turn. "If you will allow me."

Eden turned, and Falcone tied the mask back on. "Thank you."

"My pleasure." He guided her away from the broken glass and into the hallway. Falcone ushered them swiftly down the stairs and outside into the carriage.

He helped her inside and discussed the route for his carriage driver to take. After the precautions they had put in place before they arrived, they should travel a smooth journey to the assigned destination for them to meet Worth.

Falcone climbed into the carriage, and soon they were off. He watched Eden stare out the windows. Neither of them said a word. Her silence made him uneasy, but he remained quiet as part of his act.

Eden pretended the evening she spent in Falcone's arms made no difference to her. Now she was the one who lied. Their passion had tilted her world on its axis. She couldn't read Falcone either. When she awoke, he had stared at her as if he wanted to devour her. His cock straining for release in his trousers had been proof of his desire. Yet he appeared uncomfortable with what they shared.

Had she mistaken their shared attraction? Was she just another lady who warmed his bedsheets for the evening? However, the tender care he showed her by sneaking her away from Lord Chesterton's home showed her something else entirely.

She needed to settle her emotions from the passion they shared, but she wanted to do so in the privacy of her own bedchamber without Falcone distracting her. Eden had drifted to sleep in his warm embrace with a sense that her soul had settled. She didn't regret what they shared and had hoped he felt the same.

Perhaps guilt tugged at his conscience, and he attempts to act with honor. Eden hid her gasp behind her glove, faking a yawn. He wasn't contemplating marriage, was he? Oh no! That wouldn't do at all. She snuck a peek at him and caught him staring at her. She averted her gaze so he wouldn't attempt to speak with her. His bleak expression showed every sign of how he regretted their time together and how he would ask her brother's permission to marry her. No. No. No. She must find a way to change his mind.

Marriage to him would diminish her sanity. Falcone would infuriate her every day, all day long. Eden paused. However, they would fill their evenings with the amazing passion that her body craved even now.

No. She must stay firm. There was no need for a marriage between them. Now, if he wished to carry on an affair, she would be more than willing.

Falcone held his chuckle inside. He saw how Eden plotted to handle him. If she reasoned to convince him they held no future together, he would take pleasure convincing her otherwise. Or did she prepare herself to deny the marriage offer he had no inclination to ask? Either way she responded, he would offer an opposite response.

The carriage pulled up to the designation they had agreed on. Worth stood outside his carriage, watching for any signs of danger. Eden's gaze landed on him, and he waited for her practiced speech, but she didn't say a word, observing him with her eyes narrowed and her lips pinched in disapproval.

After several long minutes of silence and Worth growing agitated, Falcone decided he must send her on her way, even though he wished to spend the day trying to understand her. "Your other chariot awaits, my queen."

Even though he delivered the endearment with sarcasm, it startled Eden. Because that was how he had made her feel last night after she pleasured him. He had carried her to the bed as if she were his queen. She swallowed the retort she had on her tongue to dissuade him from proposing to her. Had she changed her mind?

"Are you not going to walk me over to my brother?" Eden asked.

Falcone lifted one of his shoulders. "It is not necessary to continue our roles. The evening is over, and we have achieved our goals. Is there something else you wish for?"

Eden frowned. "I thought . . ." She couldn't explain what she thought when she didn't understand herself.

Falcone's lips twisted. "You thought what? I would offer for your hand in marriage. We shared a pleasurable night satisfying each other's needs, nothing more. I see no need to spend our lives shackled to one another. Do you?" He arched his eyebrow at his question.

"You don't?" Eden squeaked. This conversation wasn't proceeding as she imagined it would. She didn't know how to react. Should she feel offended and mortified at how he had ruined her and wouldn't honor her? Or should relief wash over her since she didn't have to refuse him?

"No. But you didn't answer my question. Did you wish for a marriage proposal?"

"No. No. Of course not," Eden denied, gathering her reticule and pressing the mask to her face to make sure it kept her hidden. Her fingers brushed away the start of tears.

"Excellent. It appears as if the evening was a success in more ways than one." He rested his hands on her knees. "Was it not?"

"Yes," Eden answered in a whimper when Falcone's fingers slipped between the slits of her dress and trailed up her thighs.

"Perhaps we can share more memorable moments together." His fingers brushed across her curls. "I am already missing your mouth wrapped around my cock." His finger sank into her wetness and inside her cunny. "But my cock is missing this sweet vessel." He pulled his finger out and licked it slowly. "Let me know of your consideration. I am but your humble servant, my vixen queen."

Eden trembled from every emotion coursing through her. His crudity of their time together broke her. His audacity to suggest another rendezvous angered her. She fought to resist his attempt to seduce her with his touch and awaken her need. However, the way he leaned back in his seat with a nonchalant attitude, taunting her, irritated her the most. It brought back every reason she disliked the man and had never trusted him.

She refused to show him her vulnerability. Because as much as he infuriated her, she was furious with herself for allowing him into her heart. Yet she had to wonder why she held disappointment when she hadn't wanted his offer to begin with. She wanted an affair that didn't end with her walking down the church aisle and declaring her utter devotion to a soulless creature.

Eden took in Falcone's smug expression. His response was all an act. He continued to lie to her and deny their attraction. Well, fine. She would allow him his victory for now. It was best to keep him on edge, anyway.

Eden sat forward in her seat. Falcone had prepared himself for her tears, but before Eden cried, Worth ripped the door open. "Are you coming or not? If we are not home soon, Mama and Reese will discover your lie. Why was your return delayed?"

"Eden will explain," Falcone drawled, staring at Eden in amusement.

Eden glared at Falcone. "Oh, I have plenty to explain to you, Graham." She smirked at Falcone. "But I do not believe you will find what I must tell you pleasing."

Eden enjoyed watching Falcone's confident expression change to dread.

"Fine, we can discuss it on the ride. Now hurry." Worth stalked off toward their carriage.

"Eden?" Falcone's voice softened, and he reached out to grab her hand.

Eden avoided his touch. "Rest assured, Lord Falcone. I will not trap myself with the likes of you for a husband. What lady in her right mind would want to marry a depraved, degenerate scoundrel such as yourself? Not I. As for your little proposition, why should I limit myself to your bed? When I have so many other options I can enjoy. From what I learned this evening, one does not always need a bed to enjoy the carnal delights of another."

The footman helped her to disembark since her brother and lover didn't offer their gentlemanly assistance.

"Thank you for your protection this evening. Oh and for . . . Well, you know." Eden walked over to the waiting carriage, wearing another smile of victory at outsmarting Falcone.

A lady must take them whenever she could.

Chapter Nine

EDEN RESTED HER HEAD on the rim of the bathtub as she soaked in her misery. She didn't dare close her eyes because she would only bring forth memories of Falcone making love to her. From every possessive caress to each delicious kiss, she couldn't forget him, no matter how hard she tried. But in all honesty, she didn't want to forget their time together. It was the most exhilarating experience of her life.

Which left her stranded in her current predicament. Before she left him, she had thanked him for his services and boasted of sleeping her way through London for what remained of the season. Luck had prevailed for her when Graham's thoughts preoccupied him and he never questioned her about their delay. She ducked under the water, hoping it would wash away her reckless remarks.

When she came back up for air, she realized how foolish she was. However, this was her normal behavior whenever someone upset her. Her tongue struck out in anger and was her worst enemy. The marquess possessed the skills to provoke her into spewing out remarks that held no truth.

But when her eyes filled with tears at his crude statement describing the beauty of their lovemaking, she grew furious with herself. She had fooled herself into imagining Falcone was a gentleman worthy enough for her to hold pride as she walked alongside him. Instead, he remained the same pompous jackass he had always been.

Earlier, she had reached the conclusion that Falcone had lied. Their lovemaking affected him as greatly as her. Now, she only needed to figure out why he denied it.

Eden rose out of the water and dried herself off. She slipped on a robe and wandered about her bedchamber, contemplating Falcone's actions from when they departed. She settled on the divan near the window, staring outside. Her eyes grew heavy, and she closed them.

A knock on her door startled her back awake. "Come in."

Her sister-in-law, Evelyn, walked in, followed by a maid carrying a tray. "We missed you at breakfast, so I thought I would bring you a tray. We haven't visited since your sisters married Dracott and Ravencroft."

Eden smiled. She loved Evelyn as much as she did her own sisters. Her brother had treated Evelyn like an arse after their wedding. Eden had called out Evelyn when she made excuses for Reese's behavior. Ever since then, they had shared a sisterly bond and a kindred spirit.

"I am avoiding Mama whenever I can. Maggie and Noel informed me she is playing matchmaker and has picked Lord Falcone as the preferred groom."

Evelyn handed Eden a cup of tea and a plate filled with pastries. "And would that be so awful?"

Eden bit into a pastry, wishing she were taking a bite out of him. "The marquess and I do not make for a pleasant match. He is but a thorn pricked in my side."tg

There was much more she wished to express about Falcone, but she didn't dare reveal the intimacy she had shared with him. How when he kissed her, she melted in his arms. And when he caressed her, a fiery warmth spread throughout her body. And when he joined their bodies as one, she felt complete.

"Oh. I know that expression," Evelyn whispered.

Eden scrunched up her face. "What expression?"

Evelyn smirked. "You were not visiting Jacqueline last night."

Eden blushed. "Of course I was. Why do you say differently?"

"Well, the blush gracing your cheeks tells a different story. And the sparkle shining from your eyes is one a lady can never disguise. 'Tis the very same look I held the morning after Reese and I first made love." Evelyn sighed.

Eden covered her ears. "Please show me a bit of mercy, Evelyn. It is a subject I do not wish to hear."

Evelyn laughed. "I do not plan on offering any details. I only state how you hold the same faraway look for Falcone that I hold for your brother."

Evelyn rose and went to close the door to Eden's bedchamber. Once she returned to her seat, she sat forward, waiting for Eden to spill her secrets.

"We both know how that evening ended for you."

Evelyn beamed. "Fabulously."

Eden narrowed her gaze. "Not at the beginning. My brother considered himself forced into a marriage and sought his revenge against you. He was an arse, just like Lord Falcone."

"So something happened with Lord Falcone?" Evelyn prompted.

Eden blushed. Something was too tame of a word to describe the evening she had spent with the marquess. "No, of course not."

Evelyn rested back against the cushion. "Mama is throwing a dinner party on Friday."

Eden rolled her eyes. "Let me guess, she plans to invite Lord Falcone."

Evelyn shrugged. "I have not seen her list of guests yet."

Eden rose off the divan and started pacing across the rug in front of the fireplace. "Oh, she will invite him. However, she will only find disappointment when her plans fall through. Because I refuse any suit from that boorish, insensitive clod who calls himself a gentleman. He is no more a gentleman than a drunken fisherman who lives in a tavern, drinking ale for his every meal."

Evelyn relaxed in the chair, listening to Eden's tirade over the mannerisms of Lord Falcone. She held the opinion her sister-in-law protested a bit too much about the marquess. If she wasn't mistaken, Eden and Falcone's relationship had progressed much further than Mama had expected. A fact she must keep from her husband. If not, Reese would have them married within a week. And she feared Eden would need longer than a week to accustom herself to the feelings she held for Lord Falcone. Evelyn must hand it to Falcone at how he provoked Eden into a snit.

"Your expression also held uncertainty mixed with heartache," Evelyn interrupted Eden.

Evelyn paused. "Excuse me?"

"When I came in, you seemed lost."

Eden waved her hand in the air. "Yes, you mentioned my faraway look. You mistook that for tiredness."

Evelyn shook her head. "No, I did not. But I will not pressure you either."

Eden sighed at Evelyn's kindness. "Why are they so foolish?"

Evelyn chuckled. "Because they understand no other way to act."

Eden sat on the bed and curled her feet underneath her. "When did you realize what you held for Reese was love?"

Evelyn took on a dreamy expression. "After our first kiss. His kiss made me believe in myself and gave me the courage I always lacked."

Eden scoffed. "But he thought he kissed Charlie."

"Yes. But I knew who I kissed. You asked when I realized, not Reese. He mistook me for Charlotte on many occasions, but in the end, our love prevailed," Evelyn explained.

Eden pondered what emotions Falcone's kisses brought forth. They sent her spiraling out of control into this woman she hardly recognized anymore. But at the same time, they forged an unbreakable bond. When his lips brushed across hers, she wanted to melt into his embrace and beg him never to stop.

But they had shared more than a simple first kiss. They had joined their bodies together as one, and nothing had ever made her feel more alive. She only had to stare at him and listen to the husky timbre of his voice to wish for them to be alone. She wanted to know his every thought. To learn everything that shaped him into the man he was today. Eden wanted to soothe the pain she saw reflected in his eyes when he thought no one noticed. She wanted—

Eden gasped, and her eyes widened. "Oh my goodness. Tell me it isn't so."

Evelyn held a knowing smile. "If you need someone to offer your denial, then I am afraid you are."

Eden shook her head back and forth. "No. No. No. I cannot be."

"Is it so dreadful if you were?"

"You do not understand. Falcone will never offer marriage. He even stated so this morning after we . . ." Eden clamped her mouth shut, cringing at the information she revealed. "Please do not tell Reese. Please promise me, Evelyn."

Evelyn rose and joined Eden on the bed, embracing her. "Shh, dear. Your secret is safe with me. This is a matter between sisters." She rubbed Eden's back. "Perhaps you are mistaken about Lord Falcone."

"At times, I believe I am. Now he only pretends otherwise. Then other times he loses himself in our kisses. After last night, I am unsure what path to travel upon. I had considered a lifetime of solitude, but that has changed. However, I am unsure of what he wants other than a torrid affair."

Evelyn pulled back and stared Eden in the eye. "Then give him his torrid affair. Would you rather capture every memory with him or none at all?"

"Every memory."

Evelyn nodded. "Then, while you create those memories, you make it impossible for him to walk away."

"And if he still does?"

Evelyn hugged her. "Then he was not worth loving to begin with."

Chapter Ten

FALCONE SAT QUIETLY WHILE everyone in the office discussed their next step in capturing the elusive Lady Langdale. Barbara Langdale had been within his grasp a few nights ago, but he hadn't been able to do a damn thing because of the lady across from him. The same lady who had ignored him since she sashayed into the office. She greeted every other gentleman but him. He wasn't even worth a glance in her direction. His vixen had her claws drawn again.

He had already divulged the information he unearthed at the masquerade party before Eden arrived. While he listened to her report, there had been the slight wavering of her voice as she described the guests. A warm blush had spread over her cheeks when she described the reason for their delay. He admitted she was quite clever with her excuses because everyone fell for them easily. Whether they believed them was another story. Because each gentleman shot him their own suspicious glances. And in return, he showed them no reaction. Let them wonder all they wanted because he held his own suspicions of them.

Since Colebourne threatened him to keep silent, he had lost all respect for Worth. He understood why Ralston stayed devoted to Colebourne because he had once been beholden to Colebourne's biddings and he was now married to the duke's niece. He thought Worth was his own man who made his own decisions, not one to follow another's demands. However, Dracott and Ravencroft had married into the Worthington family. Worth had overlooked the gentlemen's past involvement with Lady L and trusted them to include them in the investigation. A gesture Falcone had yet to be extended.

His glance strayed back to Eden. She was laughing with Kincaid, who sat too closely next to her. She swatted her hand at Kincaid's arm in a friendly gesture, which drew a frown from Falcone. Why did she never laugh with him? Why, at every opportunity when they were together, did it end explosively? The lady was full of passion, ready to ignite, and he was the flame that lit her fuse.

Oh, but what an explosion she was. He shifted in his seat, laying his notes over his lap. He couldn't stop his thoughts from remembering how glorious she looked in the throes of their passion. Even now, he desired to cross the room and devour her lips again. Did she wear the red lip color on purpose? Or was it a tease for him to steal a kiss? Or was it a taunt at how he would never capture those lips again? Either way, he would stake his claim soon.

But if she didn't remove her hand from Kincaid's sleeve, he would embarrass them both. The thought of her touching another man drove him insane. And Kincaid, of all gentlemen, rubbed him wrong. He detested the viscount for his actions toward his sister a few years ago. His attempt at sabotaging Kincaid's chances with Jacqueline Holbrooke had fallen apart, and he had remained bitter ever since. If he had the opportunity to ruin the gentleman, he would.

Falcone realized he didn't trust a single gentleman in this office, nor did he have faith in their ability to fight alongside him. He didn't believe they would protect him if they faced a dangerous situation. But he refused to abandon the cause because of his trust in Eden. She had proven herself a reliable ally, and for that, he would remain.

"If you will excuse me, gentlemen, I must take my leave," Eden said.

Kincaid stood up and offered his hand to help Eden rise. "As always, your beauty has brightened our day."

Eden laughed. "Ah, save your charm for Jacqueline, Kincaid. She is the one who deserves it."

Kincaid covered his heart as though she had wounded him. "At least let me compliment you on your intellect. Without your viewpoint, we would have approached this in the wrong manner. You have made fine points we will take into consideration."

Eden nodded. "Anything I can do to destroy Lady Langdale. Fear not, gentlemen, we will prevail."

"Hear, hear," Ralston chanted, and everyone but Falcone broke out into laughter.

"Why are you leaving?" Falcone barked, drawing curious glances in his direction.

Eden placed a hand on her hip. "That is none of your concern, Lord Falcone. But if you must know, I promised Lord Nolting I would join him for a ride in his new phaeton."

Falcone flew out of his chair and stalked over to Eden. "Those are bloody dangerous contraptions. You will get yourself killed."

Eden scoffed. "They are perfectly safe. He is taking us for a ride through Hyde Park, not racing it."

"Still, your brother shouldn't allow you to ride in one," Falcone growled.

Eden laughed and patted Falcone on the cheek. "Thank you for your advice, *Father*."

She left Falcone standing like a fool in front of the gentlemen who would now question his behavior. He gripped the back of his neck and slowly turned to find everyone staring at him with surprised expressions. Then, before anyone ribbed him, Kincaid directed everyone over to his office, leaving Falcone alone with Worth.

"Did something happen between you and my sister on the evening of the masquerade party?" Worth asked.

Falcone ignored Worth's question and demanded his own. "Are you going to stop her? She could get herself killed riding on one of those things."

However, Worth wouldn't allow Falcone to deter him. "Please tell me you did not sleep with her."

And neither would Falcone. "And Lord Nolting? That man is a drunken reprobate. Another reason you should follow her and put a stop to her actions. He could very well already be drunk. She is not safe with him."

Worth sat back in his chair, blew out his breath, and looked up at the ceiling as if it held the answers for him. "Since you neither admitted nor denied what has shifted between you and Eden, I can only assume your relationship has turned intimate. Why else would you demand to protect a lady who only ever snarls at you? I do not need the details. However, you better make right by my sister or I will make you regret ever living. At least my mother is under the impression you will make Eden a perfect husband."

"If you will not stop her, then I will." Falcone stalked to the door, then slowly turned after he absorbed Worth's speech. "Your mother? Eden? Perfect husband?"

Worth opened a drawer, pulled out two cigars, and threw one of them at Falcone. "Pour each of us a whiskey. We need to discuss some issues."

Falcone followed Worth's orders and sat across the desk from him. He also brought along the bottle because one drink wouldn't be enough for either of them. He hated cigars and kept his unlit. They reminded him too much of the hedonistic lifestyle he used to live.

However, Worth's next comment had him lighting it up and taking a long drag. "Ralston hates these things, and I love to annoy him."

Since Ralston was one of his least favorite people at the moment, he would take pleasure in annoying him, too.

Worth took a long drag and puffed out the smoke. "I admire you, Falcone. You could walk away and never look back. Yet you stay to help fight against the evil that threatens us. I'm aware of the debt you owe Colebourne, but we both know you've already fulfilled the debt and he wouldn't damn well respond if you left."

"Your motto when I joined the organization spoke of the need for truth. I am confused why you protect two gentlemen who have defied honesty and integrity for their own means. I stay on to remain vigilant so we may protect the good people of England at all costs, even though I no longer believe in those I stand behind. I remain honest with myself, and for now, that is enough," Falcone explained.

Worth took a drink. "Very commendable. I wish I could explain my motives for why I trust Dracott and Ravencroft beyond their marriages to my sisters. They have proven their loyalty. However, I'm not allowed to disclose the information at this time. If ever. You will be the first person I turn to if I believe they are no longer trustworthy. For now, I ask you to trust me."

"I cannot pledge my trust, but I will promise my loyalty unless I see reason to break it. If so, I will give you a warning about whatever action I decide to take."

Worth nodded. "Accepted."

Neither gentleman spoke but observed each other shrewdly, each of them smoking their cigars and savoring the whiskey. Both of them avoided the subject that needed to be discussed. Falcone topped off both of their drinks before tackling the delicate topic.

Falcone cleared his throat. "You mentioned something about how your mother approved of my character, making me a candidate to be the perfect husband for Eden."

Worth scoffed. "I mentioned a variety of topics, that being the least important of all."

"Yes, well, no offense, but that matter is between the lady and I." Falcone cringed, waiting for Worth's fury.

Instead, Worth found amusement in his reply. "Oh, Eden has you twisted in knots." Worth laughed. "You remind me of Reese after he had married Evelyn. He didn't know which way was which. Just like you are now."

Falcone frowned. "How so?"

"You avoid every question I ask. Your only concern is Eden's welfare over a simple ride through the park with a gentleman, one who has an impeccable reputation and not the one you described. Your eye twitches at every question concerning if you've ruined my sister. Also, I noted how you appeared ready to pummel Kincaid after his friendly exchange with Eden. The green-eyed monster has you by the tail."

Falcone threw back his drink and poured another, only to drink it just as quickly. "Ridiculous."

Worth pulled the bottle out of Falcone's reach before he poured himself another one. "I wish it were so, but you wear the same expression as a man who has fallen. The exact one I've seen on my brother and many of my friends."

Falcone defended himself. "I only feel a protective instinct toward Eden because of the masquerade party. 'Tis all. I dislike her involvement in this danger."

Worth sighed. "You must understand, I would never risk my sister's life or virtue intentionally." After Falcone nodded, Worth continued. "Also, I held faith in your ability to protect her, and you did."

"Eden's virtue was almost compromised throughout the evening," Falcone accused.

"But you rescued her from them. What I am unclear about is your delay in our exchange. Especially since I saw you lead Eden toward the door," Worth commented.

Falcone stubbed out the cigar. He didn't find any pleasure in smoking. "I thought that was you. Why didn't you escort her away?"

Worth shrugged. "Because Eden is her own lady. She should have the same liberties to explore the possibilities of life. My other sisters live in this naïve existence they find contentment with. However, Eden is different. She searches for adventure and wants to experience life to the fullest. So why not give her the opportunity when I can?"

"Probably because danger lurked around every corner at that party," Falcone growled.

Worth smirked. "But you were her hero who kept the danger at bay."

"I do not wish to be her hero."

Worth tapped the ashes off the cigar. "Do you not?"

Falcone gritted his teeth. "Will you answer my question regarding your mother?"

Worth leaned forward on the desk. "As soon as you answer my question. Did you ruin my sister? And what are your intentions?"

Even though Worth approached their discussion with amusement, Falcone sensed a layer of seriousness he didn't reveal. Most people thought Worth was this carefree gentleman who never took life seriously. However, Falcone knew differently. It was only a persona Worth portrayed so people would trust him enough to lower their guard. When the situation called for it, Worth was the most serious of them.

"I will not answer your first question because any intimacy shared between Eden and I will stay between us. As for my intentions, I plan to marry your sister. However, Eden does not wish to marry. So I plan to take a different approach to that dilemma. I plan to woo her by different means."

Worth nodded. "I can respect your need for privacy. However, your plan sounds foolish. Why not ask Reese for her hand in marriage? He will marry her off in a heartbeat."

Falcone harrumphed. "You saw how she treated me earlier. She would balk if Worthington made that decision for her. No, I must confuse her."

Worth nodded. "You may be right. You two rub each other the wrong way. I wish you all the luck."

Falcone pointed at Worth. "Now it is your turn."

Worth wore a devilish smirk. "My mother has decided you and Eden make a handsome couple and is playing matchmaker."

Falcone looked confused. "How so?"

"Did you receive an invitation to a dinner party for this week?"

Falcone nodded.

"Well, prepare yourself for a little mischief to draw you two together. There may be instances where my mother will throw Eden in your path. It is how you handle them that will benefit your needs," Worth advised.

"Does your mother want me to ruin Eden?"

"My mother has the capability of overlooking many acts, if so needed, to achieve the results of her plans."

"Mmm. So I can consider your mother as an ally in winning Eden's hand?" Falcone asked.

Worth laughed. "Consider the entire family allies in your quest."

Falcone slapped his hands together and rubbed them back and forth. "Excellent. Now, can you arrange a meeting with Worthington on the evening of the dinner party?"

Worth's eyebrows drew together. "Yes. Why? You mentioned how you didn't wish to take that approach."

"I don't. I only wish to confuse your sister into thinking I am," Falcone answered with a smug expression.

Worth poured a splash into Falcone's glass and lifted his in a toast. "Oh, I will enjoy watching this."

Falcone clinked his glass with Worth's. "Not as much as I will."

Because as much scheming as Falcone attempted, it would be worth it when he won Eden's love. When she threw down her taunt at him today, she held no clue the impact it would have on him. It had awakened him to pursue her until she admitted her love for him.

"Now, I must take my leave. I have a phaeton excursion I must put a halt to." Falcone jumped to his feet and stumbled, clutching the desk before he fell over.

Worth came around the desk and helped steady Falcone. "Perhaps I should come along and perform my brotherly duty by stopping Eden from hurting herself."

"Yes, and I will join you to offer my moral support," Falcone slurred.

Worth shook his head. He probably shouldn't have offered Falcone the last drink to toast to his success in winning Eden's love. The man would struggle to win Eden's affections.

However, he didn't see any harm in watching Falcone make a fool out of himself as his source of amusement for the afternoon.

After all, it was what one should expect from their future brother-in-law.

Chapter Eleven

F ALCONE STUMBLED ALONG THE path toward Lord Nolting's phaeton. The scoundrel had parked it near a group of trees, but he couldn't find them. Which meant Nolting had lured Eden into the trees to steal a kiss from her.

"Eden!" Falcone shouted. "Eden!"

Falcone didn't notice the stares he garnered for shouting the name of an unmarried lady he held no relation to. Nor did Worth's laughter draw his attention. However, the lady who rose from the bench wearing a snarl did.

"There you are!" Falcone shouted.

"Yes. Here I am," Eden hissed. "Now stop your yammering."

Falcone continued with his unsteady gait until he reached her. He grabbed Eden's arm and dragged her away from the bloke by her side. He swayed back and forth, squinting at the gentleman. "You are not Lord Nolting."

"Yes, he is," Eden gritted out between her teeth.

"No, this bloke is not." He narrowed his gaze at the gentleman. "Are you trying to play Eden for a fool? Perhaps you attempt to ruin her in this scheme you play."

Worth barked out a laugh behind him, while Eden tried to shove him away. But even in his inebriated state, Eden didn't have the strength to push past him. The gentleman, on the other hand, appeared uncomfortable with the situation. His gaze kept darting around the park to see who observed them. The bounder held no courage to withstand a confrontation.

"Nope. He is no match for you, my dear," Falcone stated.

"Perhaps I should leave and your brother can return you home," Lord Nolting stammered.

Falcone pointed at him in agreement. "Excellent idea, mate. Scurry along."

Eden turned to Lord Nolting. "Nonsense. We haven't finished our ride. We both shall leave now, and Worth can take care of Lord Falcone."

Lord Nolting wouldn't look at Eden. "No. I insist you stay with your brother. No need to give gossip a reason to spread."

Eden threw her shoulders back and raised her chin. Just like the queen Falcone knew her to be, she addressed the false Lord Nolting in her haughty tone. "I do not understand how either of us would be subject to gossip when it is obvious Lord Falcone is the bumbling fool in this situation. But do scamper away, my lord. I misjudged you when I held the opinion you were worthy enough to court me."

Falcone laughed when Nolting repeatedly opened and closed his mouth before he scurried away. He leapt onto his phaeton and drove off, not even offering them a gesture of good manners. However, Falcone's amusement ended when Eden stepped forward and poked him in the chest.

"How dare you interrupt my outing with your childish display."

Falcone didn't care that she touched him out of anger, only that her touch sent fire coursing through his veins. "God, you are glorious when you are in a snit," Falcone said in awe. "Ahh, I love how your lips curl into that snarl. It only makes me want to kiss it away."

Worth slapped Falcone on the back and stepped in between him and Eden. "You have spoken enough for now."

Falcone tried looking over Worth's shoulder, but he blocked his view of Eden. "Move. I cannot see my vixen."

This sent Worth into another round of laughter, doubling him over. Which was perfect for Falcone because it allowed him a clear view of Eden. She stood with her hands on her hips, clearly frustrated with him. But he didn't care because she no longer remained in the company of another gentleman.

"Have you no shame? Or is it your intent to ruin my reputation with your drunken slurs?" Eden accused.

"I came . . . No, we came . . . Yes, we came. Worth, you tell her. Remember. Her safety. My moral support. You know . . . what we discussed." Falcone tried to piece together the reason for their interference.

Eden's glare turned to her brother. "Yes, Graham, please explain before I lose the rest of my patience and clobber Lord Falcone over the head."

Worth winced. "Ahh. Lord Falcone insisted on seeing to your safety. You see, he was concerned over your welfare and wanted to make sure you arrived in one piece. And I offered to come along, seeing how I am your brother and all."

Falcone nodded. "Yes, that. Tell her about Lord Nolting."

Worth tried to hide back his smile and failed. "I believe Falcone didn't hear about the death of Lord Nolting and how his younger brother is now the earl."

"An earl that is no longer interested because of Falcone's tomfoolery," Eden replied in disgust.

"Why settle for an earl when you can land a marquess?" Falcone asked, sticking out his chest.

"Because I have no use for a marquess," Eden snarled.

Falcone's lips curled into a wicked grin. "Ah, but your eyes tell a different story."

"Eden, my friend. I thought that was you." Jacqueline interrupted them before Eden refuted Falcone's claim.

Eden hugged her friend. "Hello, my dear."

Jacqueline turned toward the gentlemen, smiling at them, and lowered her voice. "Worth, perhaps you should help Lord Falcone home while Eden helps me with the children. I fear my governess has taken ill and I am in the need of some assistance. You are drawing a crowd of curious onlookers."

"But I came to escort Eden home," Falcone stated a little too loudly.

Jaqueline continued smiling with patience and talked to Falcone like one would to a small child. "How gallant of you, Lord Falcone. If I may impose and have Eden's help, it would be very appreciated. And perhaps you would feel more like yourself after a strong pot of coffee."

Falcone bobbed his head up and down in acceptance of Jacqueline's request. "I always knew you were a wise lady who thought of others. I am delighted that has not changed with your marriage to Kincaid. Until another day, my ladies."

He attempted to bow and would have fallen flat on his face if it wasn't for Worth catching him and pulling him back into a standing position. He winced once he realized what he had said to Lady Kincaid. Falcone didn't mean to offend her with his comment, but he probably had. He must remember to make amends to her on the morrow.

Lady Kincaid hooked her arm through Eden's and drew her away. But it didn't stop Eden from glaring at him over her shoulder. It would appear he must make amends with Eden, too.

Worth turned him in the opposite direction and started them toward Falcone's townhome. "I cannot say that went well."

Falcone shrugged. "I can say it did."

"How so?"

"I disposed of Lord Nolting. He will not pursue Eden after today," Falcone stated.

Worth scoffed. "Yes. But you have angered my sister more than I've ever seen her before."

Falcone smiled. "Exactly how I love her."

Because when Eden Worthington stayed furious with him, she allowed herself to express her emotions. They worked perfectly together when her temper flared. All it took was one strike and they would combust.

In love.

"That irritating, inexcusable, infuriating, asinine man. He ruined my outing with a respectable gentleman who treated me with impeccable manners. Not to mention the scene he caused that will spread like a wildfire before I even leave the park," Eden ranted.

Jacqueline smirked. "I believe he is a gentleman who has become quite smitten with one Eden Worthington."

Eden glared at her friend. "You dare to defend the man?"

Jacqueline bit her lip to keep her smile away. "Of course not."

Eden growled her displeasure at her friend's mutiny. She glanced around but didn't see Jacqueline's children. "Where is your governess?"

Jacqueline guided Eden toward the bench to sit. "I've sent her on home with the children. I noticed you as we left the park and thought I should come to your rescue. In truth, I feared for Lord Falcone's welfare."

Eden gasped, turning toward her friend. Jacqueline's eyes were alight with mischief and her shoulders shook from holding in her laughter. Eden shook her head and smiled. "I wanted to bash him on the head. And he would have deserved it."

"I am not saying he didn't. But you must admit his gesture was romantic." Jacqueline sighed.

"You have always found him charming," Eden muttered.

"And so have you, only you would never admit it."

"Well, I am definitely not admitting it now."

Jacqueline lifted her face to the sun. "Then you are only lying to yourself."

If Falcone could lie, then why couldn't she? His parting words the other morning declared how he held no feelings for her other than as a lover. But his actions today proved otherwise. He confused her, leaving her wondering what exactly he wanted from her. Which, in turn, left her wondering what she wanted from him. She always reached the same answer.

Love.

Chapter Twelve

WHEN HE RETURNED HOME, Falcone followed the advice of Lady Kincaid and took a warm bath, followed by a pot of the strongest coffee his cook brewed. He ate his dinner on a tray while working in his study. He took care of the correspondence his secretary had left for him to review and wrote out his instructions on the matters that needed his attention. Falcone finished the paperwork after writing a letter to his estate manager and settled in his favorite chair by the fireplace.

The silence never used to bother him as much as it had lately. He had welcomed the peace after his sisters married and moved away. They had been constantly a noisy bother. However, now he sat uncomfortably in the silence with only himself for company. Perhaps he should pay his sister Caroline a visit and spend time with his nephews before they attacked Lady Langdale. He wanted to inform Gostwicke of the danger Falcone involved himself in so the duke could handle his estate and holdings if anything happened to him.

Falcone needed to visit his old haunts now that he had rid his body of the ill effects of the alcohol. By attending the masquerade party, he hoped he had shown his fall from grace. If not, then he must attend more debauched entertainments.

Nothing caused the belief of one's actions to be true unless the entire ton whispered about it.

After visiting a couple of gaming hells and losing all of his coin, Falcone proceeded to the brothel where Melody worked. When he strolled into the smoke-filled parlor, the atmosphere was tense and two guards stood near the windows. He took a seat facing the doorway and watched the various couples exit the room and a fresh set of young girls enter, wearing their scant attire. None of them were Melody, though. His gaze traveled around the parlor, noting how the proprietor of the establishment had yet to appear either. As per her usual routine, once a new set of girls entered the parlor, Tabitha would guide them toward the gentleman of her choice.

Uneasiness settled over Falcone, and he decided the wise course of action was for him to leave. He would send word to Melody tomorrow to meet and learn his information then. Tabitha allowed her girls freedom during the day, as long as they never sold their wares outside of her house.

However, before he rose, a girl landed on his lap. And not any girl, but Lord Chesterton's bride. She didn't hide behind a fairy costume but wore a robe gaping open to show off her wares.

"Lord Falcone, we meet again." She trailed her finger along his cheek. "It must be kismet for us to meet without the obstacle of our partners. We can take to my chamber for an evening of pleasure. Oui?"

Lady Chesterton's appearance took him by surprise, which didn't bode well for his deception. Something was amiss, and he feared he would soon learn what danger lurked for him this evening. "Well, you are a surprise. Does your husband have knowledge of your whereabouts?"

She wiggled on his lap. "What Chesterton never learns about causes him no harm. Do you not agree, Lord Falcone? For instance, would your lady understand your visit to such an establishment?"

Falcone forced his lips into a devilish smirk. "Touché, mademoiselle. Perhaps we both search for fulfillment they cannot give us. But I must refuse you yet again. I am waiting for Melody."

Lady Chesterton frowned, shaking her head. "I am sorry to inform you Melody is unavailable this evening." She paused. "She has taken ill."

Falcone stiffened. Her comment proved something was amiss. Tabitha never allowed a girl to miss a night, even for illness. She always gave them enough drugs to perform for the evening. Melody's absence meant only one thing. Lady Langdale had gotten to her. He only hoped he wasn't too late.

Lady Chesterton undid his cravat. "So, Lord Falcone, like I said before, 'tis kismet. Fate has smiled upon us to indulge with one another." She pressed her lips to his exposed neck. "Come with me and I will offer you pleasure like you've never experienced before. You will learn how I can leave you with a craving only I can satisfy."

Falcone stopped her hands from unbuttoning his shirt. "Like I stated before, I must decline."

He didn't need to offer a whore any explanation. She might have married a peer, but he still viewed her as a whore.

She leaned closer, whispering in his ear, "Follow my directions, Lord Falcone. Slide your hand inside my robe and fondle my breasts. Then state how my charms have won you over. When I stand up, you will take my hand and follow me. A mutual friend of ours requests a word with you." She bit at his earlobe. "Do you understand?"

Falcone answered her by pulling her robe off one of her shoulders, shoving his hand inside, and grasping her breasts. He pinched at her nipple, drawing out a lingering moan and attracting everyone's attention toward them. He dipped his head and sucked on her shoulder.

"Lead the way, my lady." His growl echoed around the parlor. "It appears I hunger for a taste of your foreign charms."

He untied her robe and spread it open, his gaze raking her form and leaving not a soul in the room in doubt of his intentions for the evening. He continued to fondle her breasts, noticing the other gentlemen staring at them. Many of them grasped their cocks to ease their ache. When she stood up and held out her hand, Falcone grasped it and followed her like the depraved gentleman he pretended he was. However, the scene left him raw with disgust.

Lady Chesterton led them to one of the more luxurious rooms reserved for multiple couples to enjoy pleasures of the flesh together. However, that wasn't the case with this situation. Lady L waited for them, resting on a divan, when they stepped inside the bedchamber. Behind her stood two of her guards and seated in a chair next to her sat a lady Falcone had seen throughout the years while he spied on Lady L's activities. However, he had never learned the lady's name.

"How lovely of you to join us, Lord Falcone. Since you didn't respond to my message through Lord Chesterton, I thought I would seek you out. Please take a seat." Lady L pointed to a chair across from her.

Falcone followed her orders and sprawled out his legs. "My apologies. I had other matters to attend to."

Lady L chuckled. "Yes, I've heard of your exploits. I found the story of your visit to the park today the most amusing. Tsk. Tsk. I do not believe your behavior will win over the lady's affections."

Falcone winced. "Not one of my better moments. However, my luck prevailed. I did not intend to win the lady's affections. I only wished to tempt her into my bed."

Lady L narrowed her eyes. "But have you not already seduced Lady Eden, my lord? The cries echoing from your bedchamber the night of the masquerade party spoke of a lady well pleased."

"You must be mistaken. The lady I took to bed that night was not Eden Worthington. I will admit they hold a resemblance. Believe me, they are entirely different."

Lady L rose and strolled around behind him. "Now, how can I trust you when you lie about the smallest details? I know for a fact it was Lady Eden who you shared intimate relations with." Her hands rested on his shoulders and slid down his arms as she bent to whisper in his ear. "If we are to work together, I must insist on complete honesty from you. Or you can find someone else to help you seek your revenge against Colebourne and the Worthingtons."

Falcone had spent years placed in awkward situations and learned how to control his body in response. This moment prompted him to put his skills to use. As much as he wanted to cringe from the bitch's touch, he stayed relaxed in his seat, never showing her any signs of his discomfort. After observing this lady for years, he had learned how she manipulated people to do her biddings by playing on their weaknesses.

He lifted one of his hands off the arm of the chair in defeat. "You have caught me. I had hoped my ruination of the chit went unnoticed. Because it would make it difficult to keep working alongside her brother if he learned how I stole her virtue."

Lady L circled in front of him. "There is more to it than that. You care for the girl. Not a wise idea when you seek revenge."

Falcone gave a slight shake of his head. "Nay. She is but another flower among many I've plucked, and she will wilt like all the others after I move on."

"Then it would not bother you if a rumor spread of her deflowering," Lady L stated.

Falcone shrugged. "Not in the sense of it ruining their family name. But more of a disappointment. I've yet to satisfy my cravings for the innocent miss, and I haven't corrupted her as much as I wish to do so."

Lady L's evil laugh sent a shiver along his spine. "Yes. I believe we shall endure a successful partnership, my lord. Rumors of your character are quite accurate. I remained skeptical at first, considering how you've walked the straight and narrow under Colebourne's thumb these past few years."

"The lot can go hang for all I care," Falcone growled. "I no longer fit into that lifestyle, and I refuse to be anyone's lackey ever again."

"As I said before, ours is a partnership. I do you a favor, and you do one for me. Does that sound like a fair agreement, my lord?" Lady L moved to sit back down.

Falcone nodded. "'Tis one I can work with."

Lady L clapped her hands. "Excellent. Now for me to keep my silence and to silence any rumors circulating of Lady Eden's ruination, I need you to escort my friend to a few of the functions you plan on attending over the next few weeks."

"That seems simple enough. May I ask your friend's name?"

Lady L's laughter filled the room again. She poked at her friend to rise. "Lord Falcone, may I introduce you to Lady Ravencroft?"

Falcone kept his smile in place. What in the hell had he just committed himself to? Lady Ravencroft walked over to him and curtsied, holding her hand out. At least she wore gloves when he lifted her hand to his lips and kissed her knuckles. He had just promised to escort Ravencroft and Dracott's mother amongst the ton as his friend. Everyone would assume they were lovers. A lady whose husband exiled her years ago and who everyone in good standing shunned. It would prove his allegiance with Lady Langdale, pulling her into their trap.

The lady returned to her seat, not saying a word. Lady L sat with a pleased expression at how her plan fell into place. A plan he needed to learn about. Perhaps Lady L would confide in him after he escorted Lady Ravencroft to a few functions. If not, then he would use his charms on Lady Ravencroft to learn more secrets.

Lady L stood and motioned for her guards to follow. "Now to prove your loyalty to our new promising agreement, Lady Ravencroft will watch as Lady Chesterton sucks your cock. She expressed an interest, and it gave me the idea. After she has made you come, Lady Ravencroft will return to inform me of your loyalty."

Lady Chesterton materialized out from the shadows where she had stayed hidden during his conversation with Lady Langdale. She eased her robe off her shoulders, letting it drop to the floor before she fell to her knees in between his legs. At one time, this every sight would've hardened Falcone's cock. Lady Chesterton's lush figure held every gentleman's fantasy with her pert breasts, tiny waist, and flared hips. The way her lips pouted showed how they could wrap around a cock and suck for hours. However, he merely held remorse for the predicament when he only wanted Eden between his thighs.

"Enjoy your pleasures this evening, Lord Falcone. I will be in touch soon," Lady L said before the door closed behind her.

With Lady L and her guards gone, he must prevent Lady Chesterton from proceeding. How could he convince these ladies not to follow through with Lady L's demands?

Lady Chesterton palmed Falcone's cock. "It would appear you are as eager as I am, my lord," she cooed.

Even though he held no attraction to the lady, his cock had hardened. His reaction was one of a perfectly normal man who gazed at a beautiful woman on full display for his pleasure. It was how he acted that determined what sort of man he was.

He raised his gaze from her to stare at Lady Ravencroft. The lady paid them no interest, studying her fingernails as if she found her duty to watch them a bore. He scrambled to think his way out of this mess.

"I cannot wait to wrap my lips around your cock." Lady Chesterton started unbuttoning the placket of his trousers. Slowly, one button at a time. "I have hungered for you for days."

"Would you stop your babbling and suck him off already?" Lady Ravencroft snapped.

Lady Chesterton rebuttoned his trousers, then unbuttoned them again. Falcone stared down at her hands and noticed how they trembled. It appeared as if she stalled. But why?

"Perhaps you would care to help her out," Falcone suggested. "Nothing makes the pleasure more gratifying than two lovely mouths delivering me to the heights of ecstasy."

Lady Ravencroft sauntered forward. "Oh, Lord Falcone, if only you drew my interest. But I am eager to try the beauties below before I return to Lady Langdale, and if Lady Chesterton does not finish soon, I will lose out on my opportunity."

"Feel free to explore below. Lady Chesterton and I will be awhile before we finish." Falcone winked at her. "I will not divulge your absence. Consider it a secret among friends."

Lady Ravencroft's eyes lit up at his offer. She hesitated, glancing at the door, then back to him. "You promise your silence?"

Falcone's lips lifted into a devilish smile. "My lips will never utter a word."

"Very well. I shall return in an hour." Lady Ravencroft rushed away.

Falcone sighed. With one problem out of the way, he must now stop Lady Chesterton's advances. However, before he could address the problem, she wrapped her robe back around her body, flew to the window, and looked outside. Once she held satisfaction with what she saw, she motioned for him to rise.

"We must hurry."

Chapter Thirteen

L ADY CHESTERTON GRABBED FALCONE'S hand and dragged
him to the door. After peeking out to see if anyone stood
guard, she led him along the hallway.

"Where are you taking me now? It best not be another trap,"
Falcone warned.

"Shh. You will see." She led them along a darkened corridor.
Lady Chesterton trailed her hand along the wall, counting the
doors as they passed them. Once they reached the middle
of the hallway, she dropped his hand and opened the door.
She crept in and moved toward the fireplace, where she lit a
candle.

Falcone followed her inside, closing the door behind him.
After his eyes adjusted to the barely lit room, he saw someone
lying underneath a quilt. Lady Chesterton rushed to the bed
and tended to the person. Falcone drew closer, curious about
why she had brought him here. As he stood at the foot of
the bed, he saw a girl badly beaten, uttering soft moans from
the pain she suffered. Who was she? Why would anyone have
harmed her to this degree?

"Why have you brought me in here?" Falcone whispered.

Lady Chesterton wiped a wet cloth over the girl's forehead.
"'Tis your Melody."

"Oh, hell!" Falcone swallowed the bile rising in his throat.

"They learned how she planted information for your cause and beat her to send a message to any other girl who you might seduce for the same reason," Lady Chesterton explained.

"Damn. Does her evilness hold no bounds?" Falcone muttered.

He strode away, dragging his hands through his hair. Another innocent girl ruined by his hands. He couldn't escape his past; now it bled into his present and would forever haunt his future. He paced back and forth. If Lady L would deliver this message, then she had no intention of trusting him. He was just another pawn in her game of destruction.

"What was her purpose for this evening, to toy with me?"

Lady Chesterton nodded. "She wanted you to believe you had her help for your revenge. Then you will supply her with information she will use against you. She will never trust you, my lord. It is all a ploy."

"Why should I trust you? It is more than obvious you are a key player in her organization," Falcone accused.

"She trusts me no more than she trusts you, my lord," Lady Chesterton hissed.

"Yet you do her bidding."

"We all play an act to make others believe what we want them to. But I am not a fool. She watches me closely, waiting for her moment to strike," Lady Chesterton explained.

"Explain your purpose in her organization and what act you play," Falcone ordered.

"I play the act of a besotted bride who indulges in my husband's decadent lifestyle. My assignment is to lure the gentlemen that frequent these establishments to my husband's parties, where Lady L fleeces them to keep her organization afloat while she hides. She then gathers information to blackmail them with later. I am unsure of the details, but when she strikes against the ton, it will play a ripple effect with those who she will blackmail, securing her freedom."

Falcone whistled. "Quite brilliant of her. We never thought she would operate along those lines."

"She tried it on the Continent until she crossed the wrong peer, forcing her back to England. Since then, she has perfected her method. After a few successful attempts while we stayed in Edinburgh, she set out for London to put her plan into action."

Falcone regarded her shrewdly. "You still have not answered why I should trust you."

"Because I want her destroyed," Lady Chesterton spat.

"Why?"

"Because I learned she had my husband killed. She believes I am ignorant of her crime, but I am not."

Falcone lost his patience with her. "Sorry, I do not believe you." He turned away from her.

"Colebourne said I would struggle to convince you differently," Lady Chesterton threw at his back.

Falcone slowly turned back around. "Excuse me?"

"The duke and Lord Chesterton told me you would never believe me."

Falcone barked out a sarcastic laugh. "You are under the opinion I should trust you because you throw out the duke's name. When Lady L is aware of my association with Colebourne."

Lady Chesterton sighed. "He said to mention, 'Sins are but a redemption of our souls.'"

Falcone closed his eyes, dragging his hand along his face. She spoke the truth. It was a code Colebourne insisted on to trust the person who uttered it. No one knew of this unless the duke or he confided in the person.

"Do you believe me now?" Lady Chesterton whispered.

"Aye. What now?" Falcone asked.

"We return to the chamber and pretend to be in the throes of passion when Lady Ravencroft returns. I will leave with the lady, and we will report to Lady Langdale. Then I will return to the safety of my husband. Will you promise to take Melody to safety? I fear they will return and kill her for her betrayal."

"I neglected to offer Melody my protection. I will rectify it this evening and secure her safety," Falcone swore.

Lady Chesterton nodded and blew out the candle. She returned to Melody's side to whisper in her ear. Then she grabbed Falcone's hand and led him back to the bedchamber. "You must undress to make it believable," she ordered.

Falcone undressed and slid under the bedsheets. Lady Chesterton walked around yanking at the bedding. She gave it the appearance they had spent the past hour rolling around on the bed. Then she spread his clothes around on the floor. She dropped her robe and climbed on top of him, staring down at him with a pensive expression.

"Whatever your past may be, I believe Lady Eden will still love you." She ran her hands up his chest.

He grabbed at her wrists, squeezing them to stop her caress. "Never speak her name. Especially at this moment," Falcone growled.

Lady Chesterton's eyes widened, and she nodded in understanding. Falcone dropped her wrists. He didn't mean to scare her, but he didn't need a reminder of how he betrayed Eden by lying naked in bed with Lady Chesterton. They might not engage in a tryst, but it still placed them in a scandalous situation. Even though he shared no promises of fidelity with Eden, his heart had declared itself when they made love. He prayed she would forgive him for this indiscretion.

A noise in the hallway alerted them to Lady Ravencroft's return. Lady Chesterton released a moan of pleasure while moving against him, followed by screaming his name.

With a loud grunt declaring his satisfaction, he slapped Lady Chesterton on the buttocks. "Yes, you ride my cock as well as you suck it."

Lady Chesterton collapsed on his chest. "I have many more tricks to show you this evening."

Lady Ravencroft laughed from the doorway. "Not tonight, lovely. We must make our return before Lady L sends back her reinforcements. Perhaps you can convince your groom to invite Lord Falcone to his next soiree."

"Mmm, sounds like an excellent idea." She kissed his neck and whispered, "Please send word when you have secured Melody's safety." She rose and drew on her robe.

Falcone laced his hands behind his head, appearing like a man well satisfied. His gaze followed Lady Chesterton as if he couldn't take his eyes off her. "No need to convince Chesterton of anything. There are other ways we can enjoy each other's company without him having any knowledge. Your husband can be quite possessive. He only allows others to play with his toys when he desires. No need to strike his wrath."

Lady Ravencroft watched their exchange. Falcone knew she looked for any signs of deception. Once she seemed convinced, a wicked smile spread across her face at the damning evidence she held against them. One he must deflect if she ever spoke with Eden. As for Lady Chesterton, Colebourne had offered her refuge in return for information on Lady Langdale. Her marriage was a sham to where she never had to worry over a jealous husband. However, he supplied the bait of Chesterton's possessive nature, and Lady Ravencroft snatched it up to use for her benefit.

"Thank you, Lady Ravencroft, for your discretion. I shall wait to hear of when I can escort you to our first event together." Falcone smiled charmingly at her.

"Thank you, my lord. By securing your promise, you have made my evening enjoyable."

After her comment, they left him alone with a sense of doom hovering over him. In case they returned, he waited before rising to dress. Once he did, he strolled to the window and saw them enter the carriage that waited behind the brothel. It struck him as odd how none of Lady L's guards returned with the ladies. That meant one of two things. Either they waited for him to leave so they could follow him or she trusted Lady Ravencroft. He found the latter hard to believe. Barbara Langdale didn't strike him as a lady who trusted anyone, which meant her guards stayed behind to learn of his activities. How would he avoid their notice when he left to secure Melody in a safe location?

A knock sounded, followed by a timid voice asking, "Lord Falcone?"

Falcone opened the door to find a maid quivering. She kept glancing over her shoulder at another girl down the hallway. "Yes."

"Can you help my mistress?"

"What is the trouble?" Falcone asked.

She shook, too afraid to answer. The other girl rushed over to them. "They have beaten her too and have threatened her life. She has a request for you. But you must hurry. We can only keep Lady L's guards occupied for so long before they grow suspicious."

"Take me to her," he ordered.

"Take him to the Madame, Sadie. I will continue to stand watch," the girl directed the maid.

Falcone followed the maid along the same darkened corridor where Melody rested and to another room nearby. When he entered, he found the Madame's guards standing next to her as she curled up in a chair near the fireplace. They had beaten her too but not as severely.

"A warning to you too?" Falcone asked.

"Yes. Also, they delivered the same message in the other haunts you visit," Madame Tabitha stated.

Falcone grimaced. "I never intended for this destruction."

"An evil we must contend with when dealing with the devil herself."

Falcone scoffed. "Devil is too kind of a word to describe her."

"You may be right, my lord." Tabitha winced when attempting a smile.

"What is your request?" Falcone asked.

"Take Melody away from here before they return to kill her," Tabitha pleaded.

Falcone nodded. "I had already planned to. Can your men load her in my carriage while I distract Lady L's guards?"

"Yes, but be careful." Tabitha gasped for air when she tried to move.

"Will you allow me to send a doctor to see to your injuries?"

"You are too kind, Lord Falcone. But no, I cannot show any signs of weakness. I will heal in time, but I fear Melody will not. She is a dear girl, forced into whoring her body because of the unfortunate circumstances of poverty. Melody never deserved this treatment."

Falcone lowered to squat in front of her chair, drawing her hands into his. "I promise she will never have to worry over coin again in her lifetime."

"Thank you. Now hurry along before they search for you."

Falcone left, and her guards followed him to Melody's room. "Take her to my carriage. My driver will know what to do.

Then return to the parlor. I will cause a distraction, and you will keep them occupied until I can make my escape with Melody."

They nodded their approval of his plan, and he wandered back down to the parlor and resumed his previous seat. He ordered the servant to bring him a drink and relaxed with a lazy expression, watching the girls display their wares. When Lady L's guards turned their gazes away, he poured the liquor into the plant at his side and ordered another drink. He proceeded with this until the Madame's guards returned and gave him the signal to cause a scene.

He stumbled to his feet, swaying back and forth, and knocked into the furniture. "I say, have you two blokes sampled the charms of these enticing ladies yet this evening? Which one would you suggest I try?"

He splashed his drink across one of them when he tripped over the rug. The guard roared his disapproval, and he spun away, trying to wipe his shirt clean.

"Sorry, mate," he muttered and spun around, slamming his elbow into the other guard.

Tabitha's guards rushed over, mumbling about drunken lords who couldn't hold their liquor, blocking him from Lady L's guards. They gave him the perfect opportunity to make his escape. Tabitha's girls must have learned of the escape attempt and rushed over to the guards, preening all over them. He hurried out the door and slipped into his carriage, ordering his driver to their next destination.

Falcone sat back in the seat, catching his breath. He stared at the victim across him, and the heavy weight of guilt tugged at his conscience. Would this nightmare ever end? Or would the evilness that grew out of control forever plague them?

For Melody's sake and others like her, he made it his mission to destroy Lady Langdale.

Chapter Fourteen

WHEN EDEN STROLLED IN the following morning after her disastrous run-in with Lord Falcone in the park, the breakfast room brimmed over with its usual boisterous energy. She filled her plate and followed the servant to the table. Just her luck. The only remaining seat was next to Graham. She sat down and thanked the servant after he poured her tea. The scraping of utensils against the plates and jovial conversations shared between her family filled the air.

The table grew quiet once she started eating. When she glanced up, all eyes were focused on her. Eden lowered her gaze, waiting for one of her siblings to tease her. And Noel didn't fail her expectations.

"I overheard the most delicious gossip yesterday, Mama," Noel boasted.

Lady Worthington frowned. "You know I do not approve of the spreading of gossip."

"Even if it concerns Eden?" Maggie chimed in.

"Annoying sisters," Eden mumbled under her breath.

"Is there any truth to the gossip?" Reese asked.

"Why not ask Graham?" Noel teased.

Reese narrowed his gaze. "Now why would I ask Graham if the rumor concerns Eden?"

"Because Graham helped the source of the gossip cause a scene with Eden," Noel explained.

Eden took a sip of her tea and tried to distract Noel from sharing the details about her ordeal yesterday. "Why have you joined us for breakfast? Does your husband's household not provide the meal for you? And isn't said husband not missing his wife?"

However, she couldn't deter Noel. Her sister gloated. "I am here to help Mama with the dinner party for tomorrow evening."

"Also, because I welcome all my children to enjoy meals with us, regardless if they have a home of their own," Lady Worthington reprimanded Eden.

"Explain yourself, Graham," Reese ordered.

Graham relaxed back in the chair, folding his hands over his stomach, and wore an amused expression. "Oh, I much prefer to listen to Noel's and Maggie's retelling of the event. I am sure it holds more excitement than my droll explanation."

Reese growled, losing patience with his siblings. "Eden?"

Eden continued eating her breakfast. She wouldn't allow her brother to intimidate her. She had done nothing wrong yesterday. The guilt lay with Graham for encouraging Falcone. It was clear the marquess had spent the afternoon indulging, causing his drunken state. Pshh. His jealous act was a farce, and she refused to believe there was any truth behind it.

"Perhaps Noel and Maggie can share their story, and if they state something false, Eden and Graham can interrupt with the truth," Evelyn suggested.

Graham chuckled. "I cannot wait to hear this."

Eden leveled a glare at her brother, which only made him chuckle harder. She turned back in a huff and folded her arms across her chest, tapping her foot repeatedly. "Carry on."

Noel and Maggie faced each other with glee. "Well, you know how Eden went on a ride with Lord Nolting in his new phaeton yesterday afternoon?" Noel asked their mother.

"Yes." She frowned. "But now that I recall, Lord Kincaid escorted her home. I never asked why. Will you please enlighten me, Eden?"

"No, Mama. I am sure if you are patient enough, my busybody sisters will include that bit in their tale." Eden's tone dripped with sarcasm.

Maggie's eyes sparkled. "Yes, we will."

"Lord Nolting parked the phaeton on the path and led Eden over to the pond to watch the ducks. They were enjoying a pleasant conversation when . . ." Noel paused for a dramatic effect.

Eden rolled her eyes and blew out a breath.

"Lord Falcone arrived on the scene, bellowing Eden's name to a degree where everyone in the park heard him," Maggie finished.

"Then Lord Falcone accused Lord Nolting of impersonating himself," Noel added.

"Well, in his defense, Lord Falcone held no knowledge that Lord Nolting's brother had died, rendering him the new earl," Maggie supplied.

Noel spread honey on her scone. "True. We will allow Lord Falcone that small misstep. Then Lord Nolting tried to leave the situation, and Eden pleaded for him to take her home."

"I did not plead," Eden interjected.

"She begged, Mama. Eden didn't want to be left alone with Graham and Lord Falcone," Maggie stated.

Mama fastened her gaze on Graham. "And how did Graham act throughout this ordeal?"

Noel bounced up and down in her seat. "He stood on the sidelines, snickering at what played out in front of him."

"Graham," Mama spoke softly in warning.

He smiled charmingly at his mother. "Allow the troublemakers to finish before you think so poorly of me."

Mama bit back her smile at his charm and faced her daughters. "Carry on."

"Well, Lord Nolting left. Without Eden. Then Eden berated the marquess for interrupting her outing with Lord Nolting. Lord Falcone stated the reason for his arrival. It was quite romantic, Mama. He was concerned about her riding in a phaeton and worried about her safety. He wished to see her home," Noel explained.

"But Eden would have none of it. She laid into him, and from what we know, her voice grew louder and louder with each insult she delivered at him." Maggie shook her head in disappointment.

"Jacqueline was visiting the park with her children and governess and noticed the disturbance. She came over and informed Lord Falcone she needed Eden's help and gave him advice on how to cure his ailment. Graham urged Falcone in the opposite direction from where Jacqueline led Eden away," Maggie added.

Mama's fingers tapped together. "That explains why Lord Kincaid brought Eden home. May I ask what ailed Lord Falcone?"

Noel let out a squeal. "This is my favorite part of the story."

Maggie giggled. "Because Lord Falcone—"

"Inebriated, Mama," Eden interrupted. "The marquess caused a scandal because he was a drunken fool who my brother encouraged to embarrass me. Now, Lord Nolting will never call on me again."

Mama dropped her hands in her lap. "Mmm. That is probably for the best. Lord Nolting did not meet my expectations."

"Perhaps he met mine," Eden growled.

"I agree with Mama. The earl was too timid. He would never have stood a chance against your fierce character," Reese agreed.

"Will you not reprimand Graham for his behavior?" Eden asked Reese with exasperation.

Reese sighed. "I am sure his explanation is valid. I am not condoning it, by any means. But sometimes a gentleman will overindulge and in response will act inappropriately by expressing their feelings in an indelicate situation, as Lord Falcone proceeded to yesterday. I cannot fault the man for his caring intentions concerning your welfare. At least Graham was wise enough to follow in case the scene turned unmanageable."

Eden stood up and tossed her napkin onto the table. "Unbelievable. My very family defends the gentleman who disregarded my honor by tarnishing it with his scandalous behavior."

Eden stomped from the breakfast room, missing everyone's amused expressions.

Reese folded his hand over Evelyn's. "Well, Mother, it would appear you must speed up your matchmaking attempt with Eden and Lord Falcone before the rumors start to spread. Do you still hold the opinion he is the right choice for Eden?"

Mama nodded. "They are perfect for each other. Colebourne agrees."

Reese groaned. "Ahh, that explains it all." He looked at Evelyn lovingly. "Will your uncle never cease with his matchmaking?"

Evelyn laughed. "Never."

"I only wish I had witnessed their exchange yesterday." Mama sighed.

"Was Eden glorious in all her fury at Falcone?" Noel asked. The hopeless romantic in her pictured her sister fuming, while Falcone bumbled along, trying to make her see reason.

Graham snickered. "That is exactly how Falcone described Eden. To quote him, 'God, you are glorious when you are in a snit.'"

Noel clapped her hands together. "He is perfect for her."

Mama wiped her mouth with her napkin. "We must speed this courtship along. I will need everyone's support tomorrow evening."

The butler, Rogers, cleared his throat. "I am sorry to interrupt, but a messenger delivered this and stated its urgency." He handed a missive to Graham.

Graham ripped the letter open and read its contents. "I must be off. Reese, can you please accompany me to the office? Mama, keep Eden at home with a project so she doesn't come into the office. Where are Dracott and Ravencroft?" he asked his sisters.

Maggie frowned. "They are at Ravencroft's townhome."

Graham looked at Rogers. "Deliver a message to Ravencroft and Dracott to meet us at the office without delay. There is new information brought to light about Lady L that concerns their mother."

Rogers nodded. "They will not be far behind."

Graham read the letter again, his mood turning grim. From what Falcone revealed, the implications would cause a devastating impact. One that would hold a ripple effect for years to come if they didn't stop the threat of one woman.

A woman who sought vengeance with her agenda.

Chapter Fifteen

F ALCONE RAKED HIS HANDS through his hair as he paced back and forth across the office. Ralston, Kincaid, and Colebourne watched him with wary expressions, unsure of his erratic behavior. He hadn't slept because he had seen to Melody's welfare. After he settled her in a safe house with a nurse to care for her, he had sat by her bedside and spent the hours watching her suffer from the pain racking her body.

Fear consumed him now that he saw the destruction Lady L left in her wake. He had heard the rumors of the brutality she ordered from those who betrayed her. However, he thought people had embellished the rumors. It frightened him to think of Eden ever falling victim to Lady Langdale.

"Why have they not arrived?" Falcone demanded.

"Patience, Falcone. They shall arrive soon," Ralston stated.

Falcone halted before Colebourne. "You knew, didn't you?"

Colebourne gave a slight nod. "I heard rumors, but I had no proof."

"Why didn't you say anything?" Falcone accused.

Colebourne sighed. "I hoped she would have met her demise by now."

"Now she has the weapons at her disposal." Falcone started pacing again.

Ralston growled. "Weapons? Rumors? What is Falcone not saying?"

Colebourne tapped his fingers on the arm of the chair. "We will explain once everyone arrives."

"We will not have to wait anymore. Their carriages have pulled up now," Kincaid said from his stance by the window.

Worth rushed through the door, followed by Worthington, Dracott, and Ravencroft. Worth sat on the edge of his desk, while Worthington took the chair. Dracott and Ravencroft settled on the sofa.

"Explain yourself, Falcone. What did you learn last night?" Worth demanded.

"I learned how deranged Lady L actually is. We must bring the abuse of her power to an end before she destroys any more innocent lives," Falcone declared.

"Who has she harmed now?" Ravencroft demanded.

Falcone glared at him, irritated at how Ravencroft and his brother were now included in the investigation. And Worth and Ralston didn't trust him enough to explain their reasons. "A prostitute from Tabitha's brothel hovers between life and death as a result of her cruelty. Lady L has left her beaten and bruised. If, God forbid, she lives, she must endure a lifetime of nightmares filled with the horrors she suffered at the hands of brutality."

Dracott and Ravencroft exchanged a look. They had a clear picture of what Falcone described.

"Lady L discovered the girl aided you with information," Ravencroft stated.

"Aye," Falcone answered. "I do not know where to begin."

"Tell us what happened last night," Worth encouraged.

"I made my rounds again like we discussed. More of our peers showed acceptance of my return. I ended my evening at Tabitha's brothel to see if my contact had learned any more information. But as I waited, it became apparent something was amiss. Tabitha never followed her girls into the parlor, and my contact never joined them. Suddenly Lady Chesterton materialized in front of me."

"Lord Chesterton's new bride?" Ralston whistled. "I held no clue to the depths of his depravity."

Falcone stared at Colebourne. "Oh, there is more to the marriage than we imagined."

Colebourne pinched his lips. "Continue."

Falcone tightened his hands into fists. "She offered her services for the evening. When I declined, she made it clear how it would be in my best interest to follow her upstairs. I followed her to a bedchamber, and Lady L sat waiting for the meeting she requested. She wasn't very pleased we hadn't met sooner. Lady L then delivered the terms of our agreement."

"Which were?" Kincaid asked.

Another gentleman involved in the investigation who struck a nerve with him. His enemies surrounded him, even though they all held the same agenda of capturing Lady Langdale and ending her reign of terror.

"A favor for a favor. What else?" Falcone replied, his tone laced with sarcasm.

Worth sighed. "And the favor she requested of you?"

Falcone spun toward Dracott and Ravencroft. "Can you guess who accompanied Lady L to her meeting?"

"Our mother," Dracott replied with no emotion.

"Yes. And the favor *demanded* was for me to introduce Lady Ravencroft back into society."

"No!" Ravencroft growled.

Falcone shrugged. "It is not an option."

"Then make it so," Ravencroft demanded.

Falcone shook his head. "I cannot."

"She has already made this demand before. We decided it was not the best direction to lead the investigation," Worth explained.

"Which I would know if you trusted me with the secrets surrounding Dracott and Ravencroft," Falcone accused.

"And as I explained to you, all in due time." Worth stood. "We must think of how to outwit her."

"It's not an option, as I stated before."

"What have you not shared with us, Falcone?" Ralston asked.

"Lady L has knowledge of Eden's appearance at the masquerade party and of our time spent alone in a bedchamber." Falcone added the next part in revenge for Worth keeping him in the dark. "The topic we discussed at length yesterday."

"Did this occur before or after the scene you caused in the park?" Worthington snarled. His calm attitude was a warning of his barely controlled fury.

Falcone smirked. "Before."

Worthington stormed over to Falcone, glaring at him while he addressed his brother. "How dare you endanger Eden for this cause? We agreed how she may aid your cause as long as she never became entangled in a scandal. Now, not only is her reputation in shreds, but Falcone has ruined her virtue."

Worth ran his hand across his face. "It was supposed to be a simple operation. She was to go in, learn some information, and Falcone would escort her out. However, Chesterton stopped them, insisting they stay in the bedchamber he had prepared for Falcone's return. They couldn't deny him because Lady L watched to see if Falcone had fallen back into his life of sin."

Worthington grabbed Falcone by his lapels and growled. "None of that gave Falcone the right to lay his hands on our sister."

Kincaid, noticing the escalation of a fight, pulled Worthington away from Falcone and inserted himself between them.

Falcone smoothed the wrinkles from his suit coat. "Your sister is a very persuasive lady."

Kincaid swung around and smashed his fist against Falcone's cheekbone. Falcone stumbled back from the assault, slamming against the wall. He shook his head to clear his disorientation and, with a roar, went after Kincaid. He drew his arm back and connected with Kincaid's chin, knocking the viscount's head back. Ralston and Worth pulled the two of them apart before they landed any more blows.

Colebourne pounded his cane on the floor. "Enough. Everyone, take a seat. We are not Neanderthals. We are gentlemen who must work together as a team, not as opposing forces. A gentleman doesn't need to solve his issues with his fist, but with his sharp mind. Now is the time to demonstrate such."

Falcone shook off Worth's hold and stalked to the corner of the office. He took up his usual stance against the wall. As he fought to control his temper, he realized he deserved the punch for degrading Eden. He saw the reason for Worth or Worthington to avenge Eden's honor, but for Kincaid to do so pushed Falcone over the edge. His dislike for the viscount simmered too close to the surface for him not to strike back.

"We will discuss your actions in more detail tomorrow evening after my mother's dinner party," Worthington growled.

Falcone smirked. "With pleasure."

"I will finish what I assume to be correct in the meeting Falcone held with Lady Langdale. She insisted you escort Lady Ravencroft to a few affairs by showing the ton how you support her return to society. She then will keep silent and prevent any rumors of your time alone with Eden. Am I correct?" Colebourne asked.

"Yes," Falcone answered.

Colebourne nodded thoughtfully. "This is another of her ploys she plans to attempt with our peers. She used the secrecy of the masquerade party to wear a disguise to attend. While she roamed the party, she gathered her blackmail on everyone who attended. Lady L filled the party with her own people, and they drew everyone into her web of destruction. She plans to destroy every peer with the knowledge of their secrets, bleeding them dry. If not, then every one of them will face their own scandal."

Ralston sat forward in the chair. "How do you have knowledge of her plans?"

"Lady Chesterton," Falcone supplied

Colebourne inclined his head. "Yes, the lady supplied me with the details."

"Why have you kept this information to yourself?" Worth inquired.

Colebourne released a weary sigh. "Because I hoped you would've captured her before she implemented her plan."

"We have no choice but to agree," Worthington said.

"You must reconsider. You do not understand the destruction our mother will invoke if the ton accepts her return," Ravencroft argued.

Dracott interrupted his brother's argument with his own. "Perhaps we can use her to trap Lady Langdale. You know how vain Mother is, and once she steps back into a ballroom, she will forget what she pledged to Lady Langdale. The more people who welcome her back, the more her allegiance will sway to our side."

Colebourne beamed. "Yes. Excellent idea, my boy. Worthington, how soon can your mother and Evelyn arrange a ball to celebrate Noel's and Maggie's marriages with these two fine gentlemen?"

"At least two weeks. What do you have planned?" Worthington stated.

"Hear me out, gentlemen. Why not use the ball to entice Lady L to proceed with her original plan where she required the blueprints? This will draw her away from her blackmail scheme. Invite the most influential peers in society who will display their wealth. With this ball, Lord Falcone will only have to escort Lady Ravencroft once to fulfill his promise."

Colebourne focused on Ravencroft and Dracott. "Since you gentlemen have denied your mother access to your lives, she will think of herself as the queen when she appears on Lord Falcone's arm. Meanwhile, Lady Langdale will infiltrate her people into the fray when Meredith needs to hire extra servants." He paused, wondering if his plan drew their interest, then continued. "Kincaid, your men will of course also blend in as servants. We will prepare to capture her crew one by one. Once we do, her power will diminish and the ones we caught will reveal her hideout, leading us to end her destruction."

"My only stipulation is that Eden will never learn of this plan," Worthington demanded.

"Worth should never have allowed her to take part in this investigation," Falcone snarled.

"On that, I will agree with you," Worthington said.

Worth looked at Ralston. "Do you think it will work?"

Ralston shrugged. "It is our best option."

The other gentlemen agreed. Dracott and Ravencroft offered their advice on what Lady L might attempt and how they could switch their mother's loyalty. Everyone agreed about how the ladies within Worthington's and Colebourne's families would play their parts by inviting Lady Ravencroft to tea or some other function during the ball. Her newfound popularity would draw her interest away from her duties for the night.

Now Falcone understood why Worth had allowed Ravencroft and Dracott to help with the investigation. It still stung how they had never trusted him with their stories. But then, every gentleman held their own secrets they kept closely guarded. He couldn't fault them for their privacy.

As they formulated their plan, a sense of relief overwhelmed him. They would succeed in the capture of Lady L and her cohorts. With the shift in their investigation, he wouldn't have to worry over Eden anymore. However, he took pleasure at how Eden would strike her fury at Worth once she learned how her brother had removed her from her duties.

His gaze roamed the office. Every gentleman regarded him with their dislike of his actions today. But he didn't care because he had succeeded with his revenge, even though it was for the sake of Eden's reputation. He made a promise to himself to redeem his actions by loving her fiercely for eternity.

That was, if she ever forgave him.

Chapter Sixteen

E DEN HAD AVOIDED HER family for the past two days. Once her family learned of Falcon's gallantry, they defected their loyalties to his side. Gallantry? Pshh. There was nothing gallant about the scene he caused. In his drunkenness, he had caused rumors to spread of a love triangle gone amiss. Then, to make matters worse, she was the culprit in ruining two upstanding gentlemen with her wanton ways.

Noel and Maggie had taken turns in telling her about the rumors floating amongst the ton. She had refused to unlock her door to them. Eden had even denied entry to the rest of her family. Jacqueline had written to her, expressing her concern and offering her wisdom, but Eden never responded. Instead, she stewed in her bedchamber at falling for the marquess's charming attempt at concern over her welfare. Or else she clung to her fury at Falcone for causing a scene with his drunken attempt. All because he remained a coward. She wouldn't have agreed to the ride with Lord Nolting if Falcone would've admitted to how he felt about her. Instead, he treated their lovemaking as another one of his tawdry affairs.

Grr. The man frustrated her. She glared at the vase of flowers on her nightstand that had arrived yesterday afternoon, along with his note. She had thrown them out the window, but a maid had returned them in a new vase after her mother retrieved them. Then the maid had repeated her mother's message about how they were to remain in her room to admire. Eden still hadn't read his note, even though she had picked it up multiple times, intending to rip it into shreds. Instead, she dropped it back onto the desk as if it burned her. Her only thought as she held the note was how Falcone had once held the paper. Which reminded her of how his touch set her very soul on fire in a vivid array of memories.

Her finger ran along the edge of the letter. His seal tempted her to slice it open and read his charming words that begged for forgiveness. At least she fooled herself with what he had written. When she tore the letter open, Eden blamed her mother for always encouraging her to appease her curiosity.

Lovely Eden,

I know I should plead for your forgiveness for the entertaining scene in the park. But alas, I cannot. The manner in which Lord Nolting abandoned you without a care only proved my point about his character. Yes, I am aware it was his brother who held the standing of a scoundrel. Yet it is blatantly obvious their mother never taught either gentleman the importance of manners, especially when in the presence of such beauty.

Because no doubt your beauty shined like a welcoming ray of sunshine that afternoon. Not to mention how you gleamed like a glorious vixen in all your rage. Also, if you recall, I complimented you so.

I hope you enjoy the flowers. I overheard once how much you adore lilies and hoped they would brighten your day. No need to thank me for the flowers or for my gallant rescue. I will admit they are only tokens of my selfish attempts to seduce you with my charm so that we might share another interlude as promising as our last one.

I look forward to seeing you at your mother's dinner party. Perhaps we could discuss if my charm held the desired effects I hoped for.

Until then,

Your gallant hero,

Victor

Eden crumpled the letter into a ball and threw it. She hoped it would have traveled beyond her sight, but it landed only a few feet away from her. Her breathing grew erratic the more she thought about his conceited words. The letter didn't display a single apology. His arrogance bled with each word he wrote. Eden took a deep breath to calm herself, but she only grew more agitated.

A knock sounded, and Eden's gaze darted to the door. It would appear her mother didn't trust her to arrive downstairs on her own. She sent reinforcement to ensure she attended the dinner party. Eden's emotions spiraled out of control, and if she didn't settle her irritation with the marquess, her behavior would turn erratic.

She stalked to the door and threw it open. Graham stood on the other side, wearing a sheepish expression, but underneath it was also a smirk of amusement.

She glared at him and continued to stalk down the hallway, muttering under her breath every obscene slander she thought of for the marquess. "Arrogant arse. Pompous neanderthal. Drunken fool."

"Should I thank you for the compliments or is another gentleman the lucky recipient of such colorful descriptions of his character? Lord Falcone, perhaps?" Graham asked.

Eden paused and spun around. She advanced toward her brother until he bumped into the wall. "You can consider them directed at you as well as Lord Falcone."

Graham winced at the glare his sister set on him. "Ah, sis, you must admit the gentleman only held your best interests at heart. I believe the marquess has become smitten with your charms."

"What Lord Falcone holds toward me is nothing innocent but quite scandalous. You only encourage him with your amusement," Eden accused.

Graham wrapped his arm around Eden, guiding her along. "I think you will find Lord Falcone has the most honorable intentions toward you. You will see."

"You are wrong," Eden argued.

Graham shrugged. "I may be. But I enjoy watching the chase. He is correct on one thing."

"And that is?"

"You are most glorious when you are in a snit," Graham teased.

However, he never gave her a chance to respond because they had arrived in the drawing room, where everyone waited for them. Her mother usually kept her dinner parties to small affairs. However, she had outdone herself with this party. She had invited a few eligible bachelors and included a few ladies past their prime. Amongst those guests, Evelyn's family mingled.

Eden followed Graham over to their family. Her mother hooked her arm through hers as she continued her conversation with Colebourne. The duke smiled his greeting, then turned his attention back to her mother. But still Eden sensed the duke focused his attention on her, which was ridiculous. But when Eden glanced at the guests, she noticed the stares directed her way. When her gaze landed on them, they avoided her attention. The incident in the park had caused her to become a curiosity meant for them to admire.

When her gaze finally landed on Falcone, he seared her with his eyes. He lifted his glass in a greeting. Must the gentleman constantly lean against the wall with a nonchalant attitude? Was he under the impression ladies found his indifference attractive? Someone ought to inform him how absurdly annoying his actions were.

How when he pushed off the wall and strutted to the object of his desire, his long stride didn't send anyone's heart aflutter. Nor when he stopped to take a drink, no one wondered if his lips tasted as fine as the whiskey he savored. And most of all, when he spoke their name, it didn't send a shiver along their spine, causing thousands of tingles of awareness ricocheting through one's body.

"You look quite *glorious* this evening, Lady Eden." Lord Falcone's warm greeting almost melted Eden at his feet until she remembered the audacity of his letter.

"I wish I could return the compliment, but the mixture of color upon your face does not quite agree with your complexion, my lord." Her voice dropped to a whisper, not a soft one by any means but more along the dramatic way one would wish others to listen. "I do not believe your foray into beauty products had quite the response you were attempting. Perhaps you should stick to one color in your experimentation."

"Eden," Lady Worthington hissed.

However, Falcone chuckled his amusement. "I will have to convey your advice to my valet."

Lady Worthington laid a hand on his sleeve. "My apologies, Lord Falcone, for my daughter's indelicate empathy to your injuries."

Falcone smiled at Eden's mother. "No need, Lady Worthington. The injury resulted from an insensitive remark I made. I deserved it."

Lady Worthington nodded. "That may be so, but you do not deserve the lash of my daughter's tongue."

Falcone had to bite his tongue from the remark he wished to make. Lady Worthington wouldn't find amusement with the inappropriateness of it. "Ahh, but I find Lady Eden's comments very invigorating. They keep my ego in check and humble me in never underestimating a lady's intellect."

Rogers stepped into the drawing room. "Lady Worthington, dinner is ready."

"Excellent. Colebourne, if you would be a dear and escort me into the dining room. Lord Falcone, you may escort Eden. The rest can follow us."

Falcone offered his arm, and Eden took it with reluctance.

"Humbles my ego." Eden scoffed.

"It sounded better than the comment I wished to express about how her daughter can lash her tongue along my hardened cock whenever she pleases," Falcone whispered.

Eden gasped, turning bright red. She glanced around them to see if anyone had overheard him. "You must cease with your scandalous remarks."

"Ah, but then I would miss out on the lovely shade of pink that graces your cheeks and spreads to your breasts. It compliments your rosy nipples. And let us not forget how it matches your cunny when it is wet with desire for my tongue to lash upon it," Falcone continued, enjoying how she trembled.

Her hand shook on his arm, gripping him tight. The flame of desire in her eyes told him her reaction wasn't from her fury alone; it was also from the passion he ignited with his scandalous remarks. He must wait for her to express her frustration with him later. Now, he would make polite conversation throughout the meal and hope Lady Worthington sat him next to Eden.

Eden dropped her arm from Falcone, even though she wanted to pinch him. However, she must suffer through his company since her mother sat her next to him.

Falcone held out her chair. "Ahh, it appears you cannot stray too far from my reach this evening. How kind of your mother to allow me a chance to entice you into another rendezvous."

Eden sat down with an unladylike huff. "I do believe hell has not frozen over yet."

Falcone sat next to her. "Ahh, but every time I am near you, I swear I can feel the flames licking a circle around us, trapping us in its inferno."

Eden muttered a string of incoherent words under her breath before turning to her other side to address her dinner companion. A duke's second son who usually spent his time at his father's estate but had been forced to London to enjoy a season. Eden shared her thoughts on places he might visit to make his stay more tolerable. They planned an outing to the museum next week.

Eden would have enjoyed the meal more if Falcone's presence didn't distract her so much. He made no attempt to draw her attention to his scandalous behavior. Instead, he enjoyed a polite conversation with Jacqueline, who sat to his left. His only action to keep her aware of him was the slight touch of his fingers against her every time he reached for his napkin. She couldn't quite accuse him of his impropriety when she didn't know if he did so on purpose or if it was all

---

accidental. After each soft caress, she glanced at his face, but he never smirked with satisfaction.

It took all his control to behave throughout the meal, especially since Eden ignored him by paying attention to the weasel next to her. When he heard them making plans, he wanted to interrupt them and declare his intentions. However, he stayed silent so he could follow through with his plan to win her heart. Dinner dragged on. Even though he sat surrounded by people, loneliness seeped in again. The only person who mattered wanted nothing to do with him.

He couldn't help himself, but he craved her touch. While pretending to reach for his napkin, he brushed his fingers across her hand. When she never voiced her displeasure, he kept pressing his luck by stealing another caress. He noticed her glances and kept a bland expression on his face. When he would rather close his eyes, breathe in her intoxicating sense, and savor the warmth of her skin against his.

He sighed instead and scraped a fork across his food. What he hungered for, he wouldn't find on the plate in front of him.

"Either you dislike the meal or something else troubles you," Jacqueline stated.

Falcone turned his head to smile. "The dinner partner on my right appears disgruntled with my company."

"Perhaps it is because she finds you are a distraction she is unprepared for." Jacqueline smiled mischievously.

Falcone reached for his glass of wine, taking a sip before responding. "Then that would make two of us."

"May I offer a piece of advice, my lord?" Jacqueline asked.

Falcone nodded.

"Tread carefully with her. You may find the exchanges you share amusing, but Eden is more sensitive than she appears. She carries a fragile heart."

"I am aware. I only wish to show her how beautiful love can be if she opens herself to the possibilities before her," Falcone explained.

Jacqueline reached out to squeeze his hand briefly in approval of his answer. "Good. Now on to the other matter between us. I wish to apologize for the treatment you received from my husband's brutal fist. It was out of line for him to punch you."

Falcone gulped the rest of his wine. "No. It was I who spoke out of line about Eden. Your husband acted only as a friend should and defended her honor. It is I who should offer the apologies. Instead, I torment her with my teasing. I only tease her because, if not, I would cause a scandal by kissing her senseless in front of everyone."

Jacqueline opened her fan and fluttered it repeatedly. "Oh, my."

Falcone grimaced at what he had revealed. "It appears as if I must offer my apologies all evening."

Jacqueline laughed, drawing attention toward them. She smiled and started eating until everyone lost interest. "I have considered you my friend since we first met because of your gallant regard. Friends do not need to apologize when they are following their heart. And you, my friend, must overcome many obstacles to win Eden's love. You'll scarcely have time to keep apologizing," she teased.

Falcone laughed. "Thank you for your friendship, my lady. I duly return it in kind."

Jacqueline clinked her glass against his empty one. "Good luck, my friend."

Falcone needed more than luck when dealing with Eden Worthington. He needed a damn miracle.

Chapter Seventeen

AFTER DINNER, THE GUESTS mingled amongst themselves while a few took turns playing the piano. Eden tried to enjoy herself with her friends, but Falcone kept distracting her. When Reese cornered him, wishing for a private word, Eden watched them leave. Her brother wore a thunderous expression, leaving her to wonder if Reese had learned of the tryst she shared with Falcone. No. It was impossible. If he had, surely he would have demanded an explanation from her before confronting Falcone.

Eden glanced around the drawing room and noticed Graham speaking with Ralston and Kincaid. Her sisters joined their husbands, and her mother surrounded herself with her own friends. She excused herself and snuck out of the drawing room. When she reached Reese's study, she found the door locked.

Eden stepped back from the door, biting her nail. She walked along the hallway and back again. Then she pressed her ear against the door after glancing over her shoulder to make sure nobody lingered nearby. But she achieved the same results as her other eavesdropping attempts and heard a muffled conversation. Relief washed over Eden since she didn't hear Reese's angry bellows. Her brother had never learned of her secret tryst with Falcone. However, if they weren't arguing about her ruination, then what did they discuss? Was it Falcone's threat to expose Dracott's and Ravencroft's link to Lady Langdale?

Of course, that must be the reason. Whatever else could it be, if not that? She pressed her palm against the door, wiggling her fingers to release the tension that had consumed her since she walked downstairs for dinner.

"What do you suppose they discuss?" Graham whispered in her ear.

Eden jumped, letting out a high-pitched squeak. "I know for a fact Mother taught you to never sneak up on a lady."

Graham winked. "Yes, but she did not specify if I had to include my sisters in her direction."

Eden swatted at him. "You know very well it did."

Graham chuckled. "Ah, but that is not fair, considering the countless opportunities my sisters present with their eavesdropping."

Eden moved across the hall to sit on the bench. "I was not eavesdropping."

Graham sat next to her. "Mmm. I thought when one had their ear pressed against a closed door, trying to overhear a conversation not meant for them, it was a form of eavesdropping."

Eden bumped her shoulder into his. "What do you imagine they are discussing? Is Reese giving Falcone a warning about his threats? Or is he calling him out for the scene he caused in the park? He isn't threatening Falcone to make an offer for my hand, is he? No, it has to be about Falcone's threats. It must be."

Graham stretched out his legs, crossing his arms across his chest. "Oh, now you've decided to talk to me."

Eden pinched him. "You deserved my silence for allowing him to come to the park in a drunken stupor and assault my companion with his insults. Not to mention declaring such scandalous remarks of my person."

Graham smirked. "You must admit it was a bit romantic."

Eden growled. "Not you too."

"Sorry, sis. I am not one to interfere with fate."

"Fate?" Eden shrieked, leaping to her feet. "What does Falcone's foolishness have to do with fate?"

Falcone twisted his head toward the door at the high-pitched squeak coming from the hallway. "Should we check on that?"

Worthington shook his head. "No need."

Falcone nodded. He didn't wish to disagree with the earl, but he felt they should investigate the noise, considering the threat his family was under. "Perhaps I should check to make sure." He rose.

"Sit down, Lord Falcone," Worthington ordered. "There is no threat beyond those doors. Well, maybe for you, considering the glare my sister has bestowed on you since the evening began."

Falcone tightened his hands around the arms of the chair. "Yes. Well, your sister can be a bit of a challenge."

"One you are willing to take on?"

Falcone nodded.

"When?" Worthington demanded. "Considering you have already stolen her virtue and have subjected her to the vicious tongues of gossip."

"I stole nothing that evening but enjoyed what Eden freely gave to me," Falcone argued.

Worthington glared at Falcone. "That is not a sound argument to help your case. In fact, the vulgarity of it alone prompts me to discard your suit."

"But you will not." Falcone relaxed back into the chair.

Worthington cocked his eyebrow. "Won't I?"

"No."

Worthington sighed. "Care for a drink?"

Falcone grimaced. His last drink with a Worthington hadn't boded well. He could only imagine what trouble he would get in with this Worthington brother. "I had better not."

"Wise choice."

Falcone sat forward. "I understand how I appear arrogant. Not to mention how I've threatened your family by exposing Dracott and Ravencroft. I now understand where their allegiance lies and how vital they are in capturing Lady L after the meeting we held. You no longer have to worry about what I will reveal."

"And Eden?"

Falcone blew out a breath. "I wish to marry her. But since she would resist the very idea, I plan to persuade her with a more unconventional courtship."

Worthington barked out a laugh. "And how exactly will that work?"

Falcone winced. "Ahh, it is best if I don't inform you of the details."

"Because?"

"Because it might be scandalous." Falcone tensed, hoping Worthington wouldn't ask for explicit details.

Worthington regarded Falcone shrewdly for a few tense moments before replying. "You have until the end of the ball to win her over. If not, then we will proceed on my terms."

Falcone stood, stretching his arm across the desk. "Agreed."

Worthington shook Falcone's hand, gripping it tightly as he delivered his warning. "Do not break her heart."

Falcone tightened his grip. "Never."

Worthington nodded in approval and dropped his hand when another shriek echoed from the hallway. Falcone looked at Worthington in concern, but the earl only stood and shook his head in exasperation with a smile tugging at his lips. It was the first sign of amusement Falcone had seen since they sat down to discuss his relationship with Eden.

"Still no concern?" Falcone asked.

"No. Unless you wish to act the gallant hero and rescue Eden from Graham's teasing," Worthington suggested.

"I'll do anything to get into her good graces."

Worthington slapped Falcone on the back. "I agree with my mother. You are perfect for Eden. Probably in more ways than we imagine."

Falcone stopped. "I do not understand."

Worthington sighed. "Eden closed herself off when we were young because of our father's cruel treatment. The spark between you two relit her enthusiasm for life. And for that reason, I will never deny your suit. Unless you snuff that spark with your arrogance and leave her broken."

"Never," Falcone swore again.

When they reached the door, Falcone heard the muffled voices of a conversation. "How did you know Eden and Graham waited in the hallway?"

"Because my sisters have the awful habit of eavesdropping on my private conversations if they believe it concerns them. Eden saw us leave, and I knew she would follow. Obviously so did Graham. He enjoys catching them when they spy." Worthington's lips twisted into a smile. "Probably because he is the one who taught them how to."

Worthington opened the door, and Falcone listened to Eden ask Graham how fate played a part in his foolishness. She wasn't aware he stood behind her.

"Because fate guides one to their destiny. My fate led me to rescue you from a fateful mistake regarding the company you kept with Lord Nolting," Falcone answered.

Eden gasped, clutching at her heart. Why did the men in her life have to sneak up on her and scare the living daylights out of her? She turned around in a huff. "That is an obnoxious answer full of gibberish."

"Eden, please show our guest your respect. Lord Falcone only stated his opinion. You didn't need to dismiss his belief with your rudeness," Worthington reprimanded.

Eden silently counted to ten while biting her tongue. She had at least thought Reese would never involve himself in their mother's silly antics. "You too?"

Reese shrugged, wearing a mischievous smile. Eden growled her displeasure and turned to stalk away.

"Eden," Reese called after her.

She paused and turned around. "Yes?"

Reese gestured to Falcone. "Will you please show Lord Falcone back to the drawing room? I need to speak with Graham."

Eden pasted on a false smile. "It would be my pleasure."

Reese and Graham watch their sister lead Lord Falcone away. "Did you agree to his suit?" Graham asked.

"What other choice did I have? He did the honorable thing and asked for her hand after he ruined her. Which would never have happened if you didn't place her in a scandalous predicament," Reese accused.

"Yes, it would have. Those two have danced around each other for years, with Eden slandering the gentleman at every opportunity. It was only a matter of time before Falcone seduced her," Graham argued.

"Perhaps. And I will admit, my heart feels lighter that Eden found her soul mate, too."

Graham snickered. "I never thought of you as a romantic, brother. Soon you'll be spouting about love and happily ever after at the breakfast table."

Reese regarded his brother with a serious expression. "Why do you have trouble understanding how I wish for my brother and sisters to experience the same joy I have found with Evelyn? To want them to share a lifetime with their soul mates, where they share their love with one another every day."

Graham scoffed. "Because it is not a lifetime I wish to experience."

Reese slapped Graham on the back. "But that is the beauty of love. It catches you unaware and doesn't release its hold. It clutches you to her warm embrace, where your only option is to succumb to the everlasting effects it holds over you. Mark my word, brother. You are the next one to fall victim to love."

"Never," Graham swore.

Reese laughed. "No, only until after we have Eden wed. Then you are the final one to marry off. I believe I will offer Mother my help with that cause. Evelyn met a nice girl the other day. Perhaps we shall invite her to the ball for you to meet."

Graham stalked away, his mood soured by his brother's taunts. Reese's laughter followed behind him, mocking him as he ran away. He didn't need his family to choose his bride, especially when he wasn't ready to settle down.

And certainly not when his obsession with a certain raven-haired beauty consumed his every thought.

Eden waited for Falcone to reach her. She could've sworn Reese wished Falcone good luck. But she had to be mistaken. Falcone walked forward with a swagger, displaying his confidence in how he had won her family over. It appeared he had convinced them he was a charming, gallant, irresistible gentleman. Irresistible? Where had that come from? Because the man exuded sin like it was a common trait acceptable to a female's fluttering heart. Oh my. She made no sense at all with her rambling thoughts.

When Falcone reached her side, she took off, rushing toward the drawing room before he pulled her under his spell. He kept with her quick strides, not once attempting to touch her. She slowed as she pondered why his gentlemanly behavior bothered her. Eden only held fury with him. Why would she wish to prolong their return by him pulling her into his arms and whispering soft words of seduction?

Eden slowed to a stop. "Why do you not even attempt to steal a kiss?"

Falcone bit back his smile, keeping his expression serious. "I was under the impression you wouldn't appreciate one since you appear disgruntled with my very presence."

She placed her hands on her hips. "When have you ever taken my feelings into consideration before you strike with your antics?"

Falcone pulled his arms behind his back, clenching and unclenching his fingers. "The tide has changed."

"Tide?" Eden shook her head. "What tide? You make no sense, my lord."

Eden was even more adorable when she was confused than when she was in a tiff. With each exchange, he fell deeper in love with her. He wanted to experience every emotion she expressed. Each of them was more complex than the other, shaping her into the glorious vixen he desired to spend a lifetime with.

"I make perfect sense, my lady. Perhaps not to you, but to myself I do." He held out a hand for them to proceed. "Shall we?"

When she didn't move, he took a few steps forward. If they didn't make their return soon, then he would draw her into the darkened alcove that beckoned at him.

"Perhaps I wish to understand," Eden murmured.

Falcone stilled. Her statement diminished his good intentions. He swept her toward the alcove and pressed her into the darkness. "Do you, Eden?" He rubbed his thumb across her bottom lip. "Do you wish to understand how I crave to capture your lips beneath mine and hold them hostage for hours on end?"

He dipped his head and devoured her lips, leaving her in no doubt how much he wanted to kiss her. He captured her sighs with the relentless swipe of his tongue against hers.

Falcone kissed a path to her ear to whisper, "Or perhaps you wish to understand how my fingers itch to caress every silken inch of your body."

His fingers trailed along the curve of her neck to rest his hand against her chest. The rapid beating of her heart set a rhythm against his fingertips. Falcone dropped to his knees and raised her skirts up her body while his stare pierced her into a quivering mess. She was unable to respond to the passion he lit with antagonizing slowness.

"No doubt you wish to understand . . ." He dangled his next wish unfinished. His breath warmed her core with a soft brush of air. "How my tongue . . ." He slid a finger along her slit and sank into her wetness. "Hungers for a taste . . ." He pulled his hand away and brought it to his mouth, where he slowly licked her off his fingers. "Of your sweet nectar."

Falcone closed his eyes and inhaled her heady fragrance before rising to his feet. His gaze raked over Eden where her hands were spread out against the wall, her eyes lowered, and her mouth rounded, anticipating his kiss. He wrapped his arm around her waist and brought her flush against him. Eden trembled in his grasp, melting against him.

Eden waited for Falcone's next move in his seduction of her senses. But when he never stated any more of his desires, she opened her eyes and found him staring at her. Only one word described the look in his eyes. Intense. While she stood trembling in his grasp, he held himself calm, cool, and collected. Yet the emotions pouring from his gaze spoke otherwise. They showed her the need he kept contained and a gentleness that confused her. He was a contradiction from one emotion to the next.

Eden raised her hand. It fluttered with indecision, and she pressed it against his chest. Falcone must have mistaken her touch because he dropped his arm and stepped away from her.

"No, Eden. I do not believe you wish to understand." Falcone walked away from her, leaving her incapable of running after him.

Eden wanted to protest that he misunderstood her reaction. But she stayed silent with each step he took out of her grasp. Perhaps he was correct, and she didn't wish to understand. He made her ache with a desire so powerful, she feared what she might discover about her feelings for him when she did. Which left her wondering what Falcone had discussed with Reese.

Curiosity?

'Twas what had led her down this journey to begin with.

Chapter Eighteen

EDEN HURRIED DOWN THE staircase leading to the servant's area of the townhome. She must find Rogers before Falcone left. She saw the butler giving directions to the footmen and rushed over to him.

"Rogers." Eden clutched her side, catching her breath.

Rogers frowned. "Lady Eden, is there something amiss upstairs that requires my attention?"

Eden shook her head. "No. However, I must speak with you."

"My office?" He indicated for her approval.

Eden nodded and followed Rogers inside, where she sat down. She waited for him to close the door and sit behind his desk before she spoke. "I am in need of your assistance."

He folded his hands. "In regard to?"

"I need to sneak away for the evening with no one being the wiser," Eden whispered.

Rogers smiled at Eden in understanding. "Does this concern Lord Falcone?"

Eden blushed. "Perhaps."

Rogers sighed. "You make it impossible to refuse since you already know how I aided Maggie with Dracott. Also, you know how I wouldn't want you to leave on your own." He pushed to his feet. "Very well. I assume you wish to follow him when he leaves."

Eden sat back in surprise. "You will help?"

Rogers frowned at her. "You wouldn't have asked if you thought otherwise."

Eden laughed. "True."

"Since Lord Falcone has not requested his carriage yet, we still have time to prepare for your departure."

"What do I need to do? I refuse to wear breeches like Maggie and Noel," Eden asked.

"No, they would expect that. Head to your bedchamber and grab a dark cloak with a hood. Then meet me at the servant's entrance. Also, take the servant's staircase when you leave and on your return, so you don't pass any guests or your family," Rogers ordered.

"I must tell Mama I am retiring for the evening."

"I will make your excuses to Lady Worthington. Now hurry. We must prepare ourselves for when he leaves."

Eden hustled up the stairs to her bedchamber. She rummaged around in her wardrobe until she found the coat she needed. She paused in front of the mirror and stared at her reflection. Her heart raced for what she attempted. However, the woman who returned her stare held the confidence of a woman accepting her fate.

Fate in the form of one Victor Falcone.

Falcone kept his gaze fastened on the entryway, waiting for Eden to return. After he left her, he had continued to the drawing room. It was best to surround himself with the other guests or else he would cause a scandal that would tarnish

Eden's name. And he had made a promise to Worthington that he would never hurt her.

He swiped his hand across his mouth. The fragrance of her sweetness lingered on his fingers. He wondered if the sweet flavor still lingered too. God! Eden had looked amazing, waiting in anticipation for his kiss. It took every ounce of his willpower to rise and walk away from her. When she pressed her hand against his chest, he had taken her gesture as a sign of rejection. Even though her eyes told him a different story, he didn't want to force her into admitting her true feelings. He would wait until she came to him of her own free will. Until then, he must suffer through his loss with the memories she had gifted him.

Worthington followed Worth back into the drawing room. The brothers noticed Falcone standing alone and walked over to join him. He lifted his glass in a toast.

"Did your unconventional attempt at courtship fail already?" Worthington asked.

"As I explained to you earlier, your sister can be a bit of a challenge," Falcone replied.

Worth shook his head in disbelief. "Challenge? Unconventional courtship? Why must my fellow gentlemen make winning a lady's love so complicated?"

"Perhaps you do not understand the difficulties since you have never been in love yourself," Worthington quipped.

"I believe I would know enough to keep it simple," Worth argued.

Worthington laughed at him. "Yes. Because love is always simple."

"As it should be." He looked around the room. "Where is Eden?"

Falcone cleared his throat. "To avoid a scandal, I needed to walk back on my own. I expected her to follow, but she has yet to return."

Worthington frowned. "I wonder what is keeping her."

Before Falcone could panic, Rogers appeared next to Worthington. "Lord Worthington, Lady Eden wished to pass on her regrets at ending the evening early. But she has retired with a headache."

"Thank you, Rogers. I will let my mother know so that she can visit her," Worthington said.

"Her maid has already given her a tea laced with a tincture. She should sleep through the night. Your mother needn't trouble herself after such an eventful evening," Rogers stated.

"You are correct. We'll let Eden sleep peacefully. Inform her maid to let us know if her condition changes," Worthington responded.

Rogers nodded. "Yes, my lord. I will do so."

Falcone drained the rest of his glass. "I have no need to remain. Give your sister my regards in the morning. Also, please thank your mother for an enlightening evening."

Worthington offered his advice. "Do not despair, Lord Falcone. Tomorrow is another day."

"Where are you off to? Perhaps I might tag along," Worth asked.

Falcone grimaced. "Nowhere you would enjoy. I thought I would pay a visit to see if our friend is recovering."

Worth winced. "No. I would not. However, if she has, can you write out her statement of the assault? We can use it as evidence against Lady L's crimes."

"I will try. Also, I plan to visit my sister over the next couple of days. So I will be unavailable until my return," Falcone explained.

"All right. We will catch you up upon your return. Actually, your disappearance for a few days will lay credence to your downfall and also keep Lady L from making her demands of escorting Lady Ravencroft around town," Worth said.

"My thoughts exactly. I will speak with you gentlemen soon."

Falcone left and waited in the foyer for a footman to gather his coat and hat. Once he stepped outside, he couldn't shake the sense that someone was following him. He gave his directions to the driver and entered the carriage. As he rode along to his destination, he reflected on the evening. On one hand, he considered it a success, but he also felt like he had failed Eden in some sense.

He ripped off his gloves and rested his hands on his thighs. The motion of his fingers curling and uncurling memorized him. It was an act he had done earlier in the evening to keep himself from touching Eden. An act he had failed at in the end. But her simple statement had provoked him into abandoning his gentlemanly behavior. He had wanted her to understand how her very presence unraveled his control. At least he had regained what control he had when he walked away. He curled his hands tight, his nails biting into his palm.

He banged the back of his head against the carriage as memories of Eden spread out across a bed for his pleasure overtook his thoughts. An ache consumed him. The need to possess her gripped him so strongly. He pressed his palm against his cock, hoping to ease the pressure, but visions of Eden wrapping her hand around him only intensified the ache.

Falcone shook away his fantasies when the carriage stopped. He jumped out and made sure his coat was firmly closed in front of him. No need to frighten the nurse he had hired because he couldn't control himself.

"Come inside and keep Agnes company in the kitchen," Falcone ordered his driver.

Falcone strode inside the house on the outskirts of London with ease. This wasn't his first visit, nor would it be his last, not as long as he continued to work with Worth and Ralston.

A frail woman stepped out of the parlor. Her advanced age used to bother Falcone that she wasn't capable of looking out for another. But after he watched her handle the victims they brought to her, she had shown him she was stronger than most.

"Lord Falcone, I had not expected you this evening," Agnes whispered.

Falcone stepped forward, grabbing her hands into his. "How is she?"

She patted his hands. "She will live. But her night terrors speak another story."

Falcone sighed. "I feared that. Do you think I can sit with her for a spell while you offer White some tea?"

"Yes. However, if she awakens, you must come get me. You will frighten her," Agnes ordered.

"I will," he promised.

"Come along, White. I made a fresh batch of biscuits this morning."

Falcone quietly stepped into the parlor and moved toward the makeshift bed they had erected for Melody. Since she had taken on a chill from her beating, they had agreed that placing her close to the fire was her best option for survival. He sat down in the chair next to her bed. She had settled into a comfortable rest from when he first brought her here.

Agnes had bandaged her sores, and she offered Melody tender care with the pillows and blankets surrounding her. Guilt continued to rack him at placing her in this position. Her screams of terror had haunted his dreams the past few nights.

He would start out fantasizing about Eden, only to have her image change to Melody, beaten and bruised. Then their faces flashed in and out of his consciousness, changing back and forth into each other. His dreams turned into a nightmare of Eden being left for dead by Lady Langdale's cruel hands.

"Victor," Eden whispered, resting her hand on his shoulder.

Falcone jumped off the seat, ready to attack his hallucination. His thoughts had darkened into not being able to tell the difference between reality and fantasy. However, the vision before him was as real as the soft touch of her hand clutching him.

"Eden?" His voice caught. He cleared his throat. "What are you doing here?"

Eden didn't answer him, her attention captured by the girl lying on the cot. The multitude of bruises hid her identity. Her hair lay flat against what pale skin was visible. Bandages covered her arms, with one of them in a sling. She bit back a cry that wanted to escape from the horror this girl had endured.

When Eden set out to follow Falcone, she never imagined the scene she would walk in on. Rogers had warned her in the carriage that Falcone might not be alone inside the house. He had implicated Falcone visited another lady. Rogers's statement had caused her heart to ache, but she wanted to witness it if it were true. Then denying him would be a simple solution to stop herself from longing for him.

"Who is the girl?" Eden asked.

"You should not be here. We must return you home," Falcone demanded.

"Who is she?" Eden asked again, only softer this time, afraid she might awaken the girl.

"Melody," Falcone answered after realizing Eden wouldn't leave until she understood his visit.

Eden's brows drew together as she tried to remember where she had heard the name before. A vision of a scantily clad girl pressing herself against Falcone at the masquerade party flashed before her. Falcone had questioned if she had planted the information. The girl had claimed she did and then, in explicit detail, informed Eden how Falcone provided lessons for her. After the party, she fell victim to horrible circumstances, a result of her involvement with Falcone.

Eden gasped at what that involvement might entail. "The girl from the party."

Falcone nodded. He saw the look of horror cross Eden's features. "It was not from my hand."

Eden stepped away and walked around to the other side of the cot. "I never said it was."

"You do not have to. Your eyes express what you feel," Falcone accused.

"Then you read them wrong." She dipped the rag into the bowl of cool water and ran it across Melody's neck. Eden sat down and held Melody's hand, whispering words of comfort to help ease the girl back into her slumber. "Sit down, Falcone, and explain what happened to Melody."

Falcone followed her orders. He held his hands out and flipped them over to stare at how the lines ventured into different paths. Just like his life. "It is a long story that starts many years ago. However, my past has recently intertwined with my present and now it has affected Melody."

"Does your past have to do with Lady Langdale?" Eden asked.

"No. But it provided a trap we had set for her to fall into," Falcone explained.

Eden laid the cloth back in the bowl. "Which was the catalyst for how Melody ended up in this condition."

"Yes."

Eden glanced around the room. "What is this place?"

"It is where we bring victims for safety from the cases we work."

Eden smoothed her hands along the blanket. "I thought the cabin was where you hid them."

Falcone sat forward. "We did, but then we realized how isolated it was and chose this house to use instead. I hired Agnes as a caretaker and nurse for the victims."

"Is Melody safe here?"

"Yes."

"Good." Eden stood and held out her hand to Falcone. "We best finish our conversation at your home. Let us not disturb Melody and give Agnes her rest."

Falcone didn't hesitate to grab Eden's hand. Her appearance helped to lighten his guilt with her understanding of what they had to sacrifice to bring Lady L to justice. Nor would he argue with her about their destination. Because when she followed him, it gave him hope of how she wished to understand what he had attempted to show her earlier.

His love.

Chapter Nineteen

E DEN TRAILED HER HAND across the sofa in Falcone's study as she waited for his return. He told her to wait for him while he gave his servants directions. She took off her coat and wandered around, admiring the paintings on the wall. Then, she moved on to read the titles of the books that rested near an armchair. She turned in a circle, absorbing his essence. The personal effects spread throughout the room showed Falcone spent much of his time here.

She sat in the chair and curled her legs underneath her, nestling into the soft cushion as if it were Falcone himself wrapping her in his warm embrace. She closed her eyes, smiling as she envisioned him relaxing after a long day. If she allowed herself to imagine, she could picture her curled on his lap, sharing soft kisses while they offered the details of their day together. Did she imagine the impossible? Or did she allow her determination to stay unmarried to stop her from a passion-filled life with Falcone?

Falcone stood inside the door, leaning against the woodwork as he gazed upon Eden. She sat peacefully in his favorite armchair. He knew she wasn't asleep, only resting. He wondered if she pictured them together, enjoying a moment together before their children ran into the room, playing with each other. Falcone had gotten ahead of himself, but that was what happened when one dreamed. Also, he longed for commotion to replace the silence he lived in. A wife and children would be the perfect solution. But only if Eden was his wife. He would settle for no other.

Eden opened her eyes when she felt Falcone staring at her. He had discarded his suit coat and cravat. She smiled when she saw him standing in his usual stance. It used to irritate her when he displayed such arrogance. Now the start of desire stirred within her. When he pushed off the wall and strolled toward her, the stirring swiftly changed to a fluttering. Falcone lifted her effortlessly and sat back down with her curled on his lap, just as she had imagined.

She cupped his cheek, resting her forehead against his. "Will you tell me everything?"

Falcone nodded, and Eden pressed a soft kiss against his lips before laying her head on his chest. Somewhere between the dinner party and his visit to check on Melody, their relationship had shifted. In truth, it had happened even before he left the Worthington home. He just hadn't been aware of it. When he left Eden standing in the hallway, he had thought she would never admit to her feelings for him. Now she sat nestled in his arms, wanting to learn every detail of his existence without judgement. However, he refused to question why or how. He only accepted her change of mind as another gift she bestowed on him.

"A few years ago, I led what most would describe as a hedonistic lifestyle filled with every debaucherous act one might imagine. I didn't care about anything but how the next day I could become more depraved," Falcone started.

"May I ask why?" Eden whispered.

"No particular reason. Boredom. Adventure. Amusement. It amazed me how sinful I could be and how the ton still considered me a catch. How they shielded their eyes when it would benefit them. You saw for yourself at the masquerade party how unsavory many of our peers are," Falcone explained.

"What changed?" Eden toyed with the buttons on his vest.

Falcone stiffened under Eden. "An unfortunate incident that caused the death of an innocent girl." He took a deep breath. "While enjoying myself at one of Lord Chesterton's parties, I lured a girl into the bedchamber for an evening of sinful pleasures. After pressuring her to enjoy a few glasses of wine, I started my seduction. Only the girl passed out. Since I overindulged myself, I fell asleep next to her. When I came to a few hours later, I thought to try again, especially since we lay naked together. But to my horror, the girl no longer lived."

Falcone paused, taking deep breaths to calm himself as he relived the horror from that night and tackled the guilt that continued to haunt him. Eden's faint whispers of comfort drifted through to settle his tortured thoughts.

"I jumped out of bed, panicking about the implications I must deal with. The guilt lay with me since I lured her away from the party to steal her innocence. I saw the life I had become accustomed to ripping away. It was what I deserved, but I was a selfish bastard who refused to relinquish my pampered life. So, as the coward I was, I fled before anyone came upon us," Falcone continued.

"Where did you go?"

Falcone pressed a kiss on Eden's head. He felt relief when she hadn't leapt from his lap in horror of his actions. Yet she still might. "Rumors circulated of a peer with a powerful reach who held the ability to cause incidents to disappear. However, you must pay the price of his demands for however long he seemed fit. A price I continue to pay."

"Colebourne," Eden declared as if she knew the duke's agenda firsthand.

Falcone tipped Eden's chin in his direction. "How do you know he is the peer I refer to?"

"Pshh, you are not the only one under his direction. His reach extends far beyond what we imagine."

He gripped her shoulders. "Even to you?"

Eden snuggled back against his chest. "No. Now, continue with your story. I have plans for you, Lord Falcone."

His heart filled with her promise and gave him hope that he didn't frighten her away with the truth of his past. "Demanding, like always." He smiled when she chuckled, then turned serious again. "I went to Colebourne. He promised he would look into the matter and make it disappear forever. In return, I would do his bidding whenever he demanded. Even so far as to stay quiet on certain topics if he so wishes. His final stipulation was to walk away from the life I led and start a more honorable one."

"Do you follow his demand to stay silent in regard to Dracott and Ravencroft?" Eden inquired.

"Yes. At first, I was furious at the request, and to be honest, it stung my pride. I'd thought I was a trusted ally with Worth and Ralston. And when they wouldn't confide in me, it only tightened the reins Colebourne kept me in. I wanted revenge for them not trusting me. However, I've since learned how valuable Dracott and Ravencroft are to the organization and realized they are allowed their secrets, as I am mine."

Eden unbuttoned his vest. "We shall return to the revenge part, but for now, tell me about the girl."

"She was the sister of a gentleman who visited the same haunts as I did. Their family had fallen on hard times after their parents died in a carriage accident. The brother had neglected the sister. On that evening, she followed him into his life of sin, unaware of what she walked into. Her innocence attracted me and so I lured her into my den of depravity, unaware of her circumstances. Colebourne discovered the girl suffered from a heart condition and wanted to experience an evening of entertainment instead of lying in a sickbed. When I thought she had passed out, it was because the wine she drank caused her heart to stop beating," Falcone explained.

"Because of the amount?"

Falcone shook his head sadly. "No. Colebourne also discovered someone had laced the wine with opium. A normal occurrence at these parties. I never thought differently when I drank the wine."

"Did her brother ever learn of your involvement with his sister's death?"

"No, because the following morning, he died in a duel. A furious husband discovered his wife's infidelity and avenged his honor. Which left an elderly aunt to grieve the unfortunate deaths of her kin. One death should never have happened. I wear the scars on my hands for the part I played," Falcone finished.

Eden heard the guilt that weighed heavily on Falcone with every regretful word he spoke. She cupped his cheeks and stared into his eyes. "That girl did not die at your hands. She died as a result of unfortunate circumstances. Events led her to you, combined with other factors you had no control over. I believe the girl already knew her fate and wanted the chance to experience life before it slipped away from her. Your interest, as depraved as it might have been, probably made her feel special before she took her last breath."

Falcone wiped the tears away from Eden's cheeks. "I wish I held the same belief, but as long as my nightmares remind me of my sins, I cannot believe otherwise."

"One day you will, I promise," Eden whispered.

Her promise helped to soothe a part of his soul. His love for her gave him the strength to overcome his demons. If she were to declare her love for him, it would make him whole.

"It suffocated me when Worth and Ralston forced me to return to my old lifestyle. A heavy weight sat on my chest at the sickness I once relished in. I tried so hard to get you out of that masquerade party."

Eden kissed his palm. "The bedchamber Lord Chesterton forced us into was the same one where your life changed forever. And the reason you fought making love to me."

Falcone huffed out a breath. "You made it very difficult for me to refuse."

Eden smiled seductively. "That was because you seduced me all evening, only to change your mind. Sometimes a lady must persuade a gentleman to change his mind."

Falcone growled, shifting Eden on his lap. "You may practice your art of persuasion on me whenever the fancy strikes you."

Eden slapped his chest. "We have not finished our discussion yet."

Falcone chuckled. "Then what is the next topic you wish to hear about?"

"Melody."

The one name that made their playfulness disappear, but one they must discuss. "On one of my visits to an old haunt, Melody approached me."

"Propositioned you most likely," Eden muttered.

Falcone smiled at her jealous tone. "Yes, you are correct. Anyway, I convinced her if she were to help plant some information, I would make it worth her efforts." Eden stiffened under him, and he realized he must make his intentions clearer. "As in enough money, so she no longer needed to sell her body for coin. However, she took it to mean something else entirely."

"That was more than obvious," Eden spat.

Falcone sighed. "And I never attempted to state otherwise. My only objective was to relay false information to Lady Langdale, the rest I would clarify when the time came. Unfortunately, I was too late. Lady L learned of the deceitful information and taught Melody and the madame of the brothel a lesson about their betrayal."

He hated to lie to Eden since her visit showed proof of how she wanted to explore where their attraction might lead. As much as he wanted to tell her the details that had led to him discovering the brutality Melody suffered from, he couldn't. They had decided in their meeting to keep Eden in the dark for the rest of the investigation to protect her, which meant she could never learn of his arrangement with Lady L concerning Lady Ravencroft until the night of the ball. Falcone would admit the truth and pray for Eden's forgiveness after they captured Lady Langdale. He would do anything to keep her from suffering the same fate as Melody.

"So, you brought Melody to the safe house, where Agnes is tending her wounds. What will happen to Melody if she recovers?"

Falcone slipped the pins from Eden's hair, letting them drop on the rug. "I have made arrangements for her to move to a cottage wherever she may choose to live. I will provide for her remaining life."

Eden unbuttoned Falcone's shirt, slipping her hand inside to stroke across his chest. "Now, shall we discuss the bit of revenge you planned to seek? It wouldn't, by any chance, have anything to do with me?"

Falcone ran his hand through her luxurious curls. "It revolved entirely around you."

Eden pressed her lips to his neck as she inhaled his masculine scent. "And did you find much success with your revenge?"

Falcone closed his eyes at the seductive pull of her lips against his. "What revenge?" he murmured.

Eden changed her position on his lap to where she straddled him. He threw his head back over the edge of the chair, and his face held the expression of a man enjoying the pleasure of a woman. Eden shifted, pressing her core against his cock and earning a moan from Falcone. She ran her hands along his chest and into his hair as her mouth hovered a whisper away from his.

"Exactly," she declared before devouring him with a kiss.

Chapter Twenty

EDEN HAD WAITED LONG enough to taste him. To show him she understood what he longed for, because she longed for the same. But it wasn't only about the attraction that always simmered between them. It went much deeper than she believed they understood. All these years, she didn't dislike him because of his arrogance and how he regarded her. He had pulled her to him with every smirk and irritating remark, and for that, she fought against him. She had allowed her fear of exposing her vulnerability keep her from this man.

Falcone only allowed her the one possessive kiss before he rose with her in his arms and carried her to his bedchamber. Their lips never broke apart once except for soft moans escaping their drawn breaths before kissing once again. He slid her along his body, molding her soft curves to his hard ridges.

Falcone turned Eden around and slowly stripped the clothes from her body, brushing soft kisses across her exposed skin. As much as she wanted to rush them along, she enjoyed his gentleness too much to demand otherwise. Once he divested her clothing, he pressed against her back and cupped her breasts. He bent his head, drawing a path of fire along her neck with his gentle kisses, while his fingers pinched at her buds with the softest of touches.

"Do you have any clue how glorious you are, my vixen?" he whispered in her ear before dipping one of his hands between her curls to stroke her wetness.

Eden's knees buckled at all the delicious sensations of Falcone's attention. He lifted her and laid her on the bed. She watched him as he impatiently tore off his clothes, the complete opposite of how he had discarded hers. It brought a wanton smile to her lips; she enjoyed the effect she held over him. She lifted her arms above her head and stretched her body out on his sheets.

Falcone growled at Eden's sensual pose. The vixen realized the power she held over his senses and set out to tease him with her voluptuous body. Her back arched while she stretched. Her breasts were like beacons of light, directing him to start his seduction by suckling her buds until her moans of desire filled his bedchamber. But as his gaze traveled along her silken limbs, her wetness glistened on her curls, demanding that he satisfy their hunger with his ravenous appetite.

"Falcone." Eden's husky whisper made its own demand.

"Victor," he growled.

"Falcone," Eden teased.

His gaze pierced her until the teasing glint in her eyes changed to hunger. He wrapped his hands around her ankles and pulled her toward him in one tug. At her gasp, he spread her thighs apart, dipped his head to her core, and blew a harsh breath across her wetness. At her moan, he drug his tongue along her folds and devoured her. He had hungered for a taste of her since his fingers teased her earlier. When he licked her off his fingers, he had tormented himself more than he had her.

Falcone's groan vibrated against her core, intensifying the pleasure he gifted her. Her fingers sank in his hair and held him to her core. She pressed herself into his mouth as his tongue struck against her with one powerful lash after another. But still it wasn't enough. Her body ached with a need unknown to her. However, Falcone understood how to ease the ache consuming her. He teased her into a quivering mess until she begged him to help her.

"Please, Falcone," Eden whimpered.

Falcone lifted his head to watch Eden unravel. His fingers replaced the torment of his mouth with swift strokes in and out of her pussy, while his thumb circled her clit. "I cannot, sweet Eden."

"Please, you must," Eden begged.

He lowered his head to tease her with one lick. "You know what I request of you."

His request was simple enough. But Eden had to admit to herself that she refused to fulfill it because she loved how her body responded to him and never wanted it to end. She loved the highs he delivered with each stroke of his tongue, and she loved the lows when he teased her with his refusal. Even now, his mouth caressed along her thighs to the crease of her legs, avoiding her need. It drove her wild.

Eden was a mixture of enchanting contradictions. And he loved every single one of them to a point of madness. With each kiss, he savored the tasty morsel of her desires, a flavor he had become addicted to. The demand to hear his request slipped from his control. Falcone no longer held the power to resist her pleas.

He pulled her to his mouth and struck out relentlessly until she screamed her pleasure. And still he never relented. Each stroke became more demanding as he licked at her cream. Even when she shouted, "Victor. Victor," over and over, he continued.

Eden floated, trembling from the pleasure Victor gave her. Still, he lay between her thighs, his head nestled against her curls, while he built the ache into an all-consuming passion over and over. Each time she felt herself falling, he would catch her and lay her on a cloud to float while he sent her falling off the edge again.

Victor caught her, worshipping her body with soft kisses while she floated back to him. His head rested against her breasts, suckling on her buds. His tongue traced the soft pink nipple before drawing it between his lips. When he dragged his teeth across her nipple, the familiar moan of her need sang a soft melody.

He rose above her and entered her slowly as he watched the cloudy mist of desire swirl in her eyes. Each stroke in and out drove his need to roar at the pleasure she gave him. He whispered, "That wasn't so difficult, was it?" then pressed deep enough into her core to draw out a gasp from her lips as he rolled them over.

Eden gasped for air at the delicious sensations coursing through her at each stroke of his cock inside her. The arrogant smile on his face only built her desire. However, he must learn how his smirk held consequences. As much as she enjoyed the tingles that zinged through her core, she must teach Victor a lesson. What did it matter if she found pleasure from the lesson too? It was one she must teach.

Eden slid her body down the length of him, her nipples brushing across his hard ridges along the way until she settled between his legs. "It wasn't difficult at all."

Her hand enclosed his cock in her warm grip, sliding it up and down with her thumb and brushing across the tip. "What should it matter if I call out . . ." Her mouth drew him inside her mouth deeply, then pulled him out, stroking him again. "Falcone in the throes of passion . . ." Her mouth lowered and repeated the same action again. "Or Victor?" She pressed her tongue against his cock, drawing him in deeper.

Victor was the one who gasped for air now. His fingers clenched the bedsheets as Eden tormented him in the sweetest way possible. Her tongue teased him with soft licks while her mouth sucked him with greed. Her question became lost in his hazy thoughts.

"Also, we should address the appropriate moments when you should or should not smirk at me, Lord Falcone." Eden swirled her tongue around the tip, savoring his wetness. She drew the head of his cock between her lips and softly sucked on him. "It is quite rude of you to smirk your arrogance after you brought me to the pinnacle of heightened pleasure."

She never gave him a chance to respond before she drew him back into her mouth and slid him in and out, taking him to the same pinnacle he had taken her. His cock throbbed in her mouth with his need.

Victor could take no more. She had him at her mercy. The need to explode beat against her tongue, but the need to sink into her warmth and share his pleasure with her beat stronger. He drew her up his body and flipped her underneath him. The coy smile gracing her face would be his demise, one he would welcome with open arms.

He pressed into her slowly and gently, drawing the tension out. "My deepest . . ." He pressed deeper. "Apologies, Lady Eden, for my conceit. I will refrain from smirking at you . . ." He pulled out and slid in harder. "While I make . . ." He pulled out again, only this time he slid inside her so deliberately to make his point. "*Love* to you."

Eden's gaze darkened at his apology. He drew her body closer and kissed her as he made love to her. Their bodies intertwined as their souls merged into one with each powerful stroke. Victor loved this woman more than he thought possible.

Eden clung to Victor as he sent them soaring, her heart filled with love for him. She now understood what he had meant earlier about the tide changing. It was a metaphor for the shifting of their feelings for one another. How he no longer wished to clash with her but to explore the dynamics of their attraction. Only it went so much deeper than they ever imagined. It all revolved around the matters of their hearts.

Victor gathered Eden close. His hand stroked along her body, his need to continue touching her held strong. He savored the time with her, aware that it would soon end. He must return her to the safety of her family before the sun rose. He wished for nothing more than to watch the sunrise with her while she lay in his embrace. But he would remain patient for that day to come.

"Victor," Eden murmured.

"Mmm." His fingers stroked across her breast.

Eden rolled across his chest and brushed the hair off his forehead. "You may smirk whenever you please."

Victor laughed, squeezing her in a hug. "As long as you promise to snarl at me every once in a while."

"Mmm." Eden placed soft kisses across his chest. Who knew their smirks and snarls had been what attracted them to each other? "I believe I can make that promise possible."

"Eden?"

"Shh." She placed her finger over his lips. She wasn't ready for emotional declarations of love yet.

Victor kissed her finger. He understood her fear of laying her heart open for him to steal. Just the act of her lying in his arms at this moment showed him how she attempted to conquer her fear. He would give her the time she needed to understand he wasn't stealing her heart but guarding it as the precious gem it was. Until then, he would remain steadfast in his patience and show her how special she was to him.

Victor's act of following her request only broke down her defenses with him more. Why had she never seen how truly gallant he was? Every other lady she surrounded herself with saw how honorable he was. But she had foolishly convinced herself he played everyone false with his charm. Even now she resisted his gallant offer of remaining quiet with expressing his emotion, believing it to be another flaw in his character when her heart vastly objected.

Her fingers traced over the bruising on his cheek. "Who did you anger?"

Victor closed his eyes at her touch. "Kincaid."

Eden pressed a kiss against his injury. "Why?"

He opened his eyes to stare into hers as he confessed how he had tarnished her name. "Because I boasted about how I couldn't refuse your persuasive offer of pleasure."

"Oh." Eden withdrew her fingers. "As part of your revenge?"

"No. Since the first time I drew your body underneath mine, my thirst for revenge ended. I acted like an arse because they wanted me to take blame for your appearance at the masquerade party, when it was Worth who pushed the issue and disregarded my warnings," Victor explained. "I apologize for slandering your good name."

Eden nodded, folding her hands on his chest, and stared at him. She heard the sincerity of his explanation and understood why he had acted out. "I need to return home."

Victor nodded in agreement but wouldn't release his hold. Nor did Eden try to rise. She didn't wish to part from him with this clouding over them.

"I forgive you, Victor. However, I am troubled by this animosity that remains between you and Lord Kincaid."

"He involved my sister in a scandal because of his sheer boredom with life," Victor snarled.

Eden traced her fingers around his lips to ease away their tight hold. "Did you ever take my advice and ask your sister what happened between her and Lord Kincaid?"

"No," Victor growled. "I don't need her explanation to know how he jeopardized her marriage and slandered her good name for a bit of fun."

Eden kissed him before pulling away. "I wish you would speak with her. At least to understand what occurred. After that, if she confirms what you believe to be true, then I shall stand by your side and share your beliefs."

Victor let her slip from his grasp and watched her while she gathered her clothes. He never replied to her request because he didn't wish to discuss this sensitive subject with his sister. Over the years, he had watched her marriage flourish. He never wanted to recall the past and cause a disturbance that should've stayed forgotten.

When Eden struggled with her dress, he sat up, pulled her between his legs, and finished closing the buttons together. He wrapped his arms around her waist and pressed his cheek to her back. He didn't want to let her go. They still had so much to share with one another.

Eden closed her eyes, enjoying their tender embrace. What she wouldn't do to coax him back under the bedsheets. To ease his troubled soul with her affectionate caresses. To kiss away every terror that haunted him. So instead of easing the conflicts that consumed him, she turned in his arms and offered him a bit of humor instead. Her heart was too vulnerable to act in any other accord. "Persuasive, you say?"

Victor chuckled. "Mmm. Very much so."

Eden bounced away, wearing a smirk. "That is interesting to know."

"Is that so?" Victor pulled her into his arms again.

"Yes. It is." She sighed into his kiss, wrapping her arms around his neck.

Victor didn't care how she held the knowledge to bring him to his knees, only that she would once again try. He reluctantly pulled away from their kiss to dress for her return home.

During the carriage ride, he held her. He waited until they reached the mews behind her home before he told her of his plans. "I am leaving town for a few days. I've made plans to visit my sister and her family. Please do not think that I've abandoned you," Victor expressed.

"And on your return?" Eden questioned.

Victor spoke from the heart. "I hope you will accept my suit."

"And if I chose not to, will you respect my wishes?"

"No. I will try to persuade your affections with my gallant charms," Victor declared.

Eden tried to hide her smile at his declaration but failed. "Mmm."

Victor took her murmured response as a positive sign of their future together. "May I ask for a promise to my next request?"

"Explain it, and we shall see."

"Can you please keep from visiting Worth's office while I am away? Lady L has knowledge of your identity and has made threats to expose your visit to the masquerade party. I do not wish to worry over your safety during my absence and would feel much better if you stayed close to home. I fear she will strike against you in the same manner she did Melody."

Eden squeezed his hands. "If I can ease your mind during your absence, I promise to stay away from Worth's office."

"There is more I must confess and I hope you do not see it as a betrayal on my part or your brother's part. We have contrived a plan to capture Lady L and her gang."

Eden pinched her lips at learning they had excluded her from the discussion. "And that plan might be?"

Victor winced at Eden's hurt expression. "A ball held in your home to celebrate Noel's and Maggie's marriages. Since we all want you to stay as safe as possible, we hoped you would help your mother with the plans for the ball. You can implement the needs for us to capture Lady Langdale. Worth will speak with you tomorrow morning about how you can help by organizing the ball. You are still a vital part of this plan, just in a different capacity than what you've been in the past."

What he neglected to tell her was who he would escort to the ball. They had all agreed it was best to keep Eden in the dark. That way, the element of surprise would be a genuine reaction, showing proof of his deception.

Eden pulled away. "I will only agree if you agree to my stipulation."

Victor narrowed his gaze. "And that would be?"

Eden offered him a deal to seal her agreement. "I will remain close to home and help my mother plan a ball that is really meant for a capture if you in exchange discuss with your sister the circumstances of her involvement with Lord Kincaid."

"Absolutely not," Victor growled. "I already explained my reasons to you for not discussing this with her."

Eden patted the bruise on his cheek. "Then we do not have a deal."

"Damn you," Victor muttered.

Eden taunted him with her cheeky smile before opening the door to the carriage. "Do make a call on your return. I would love to hear about your visit with your family."

Victor followed her through the garden to make sure she made it inside safely. Before they reached the house, he swung her around and pressed her against a tree. "Fine. I accept your demand."

Eden slid her arms around his waist. "That was not so difficult, was it, Lord Falcone?"

As he said before, the vixen could be more than persuasive.

Chapter Twenty-One

F ALCONE THREW HIMSELF ONTO the chair next to his sister, laughing over his nephews' antics. He had arrived at his sister's estate the evening before, and his nephews had dragged him out at dawn to go fishing, then swimming, finally ending their day with a game of chase through the garden. "Where do they find the energy?"

Caroline laughed. "I assume the same place you used to find it. You drove Mother mad with your exuberance."

Falcone chuckled. "Yes, I suppose I did." He watched the boys with a fondness he had never appreciated before.

"You need a couple of those yourself. Perhaps you should approach the season with seriousness and find a gracious lady to marry. But of course, she must not be too nice where she tolerates your arrogance," Caroline suggested.

Falcone grinned at her. "Perhaps I've already met the lady who meets that criteria."

Caroline frowned at him. "I am being serious."

Falcone popped a grape into his mouth. "As am I."

"Seriously?" she asked.

Falcone nodded, focusing his attention back on his nephews. He wondered if his and Eden's children would hold the same carefree exuberance as them.

Caroline sat back in her chair and continued with her knitting. "Who is she?"

"Eden Worthington." A smile lit his face whenever he mentioned her name.

Caroline gasped. "I thought she detested the very sight of you. And doesn't she annoy you with her criticisms of your character? Why, on your last visit, you carried on and on about how she snarled at you whenever you spoke. I must admit, I was more than thrilled when you left. I didn't have to endure listening to you say, 'The nerve of that woman,' over and over."

Falcone offered his sister a sheepish expression. "Yes. We seem to have discovered that underneath all our hatred burns a passion unlike anything imaginable."

"You love her," Caroline said in awe.

"Yes."

The click-clack of the needles as Caroline fed the yarn filled the silence. He stared at his sister as she knitted and watched her children play with a smile gracing her face. It frustrated him all those years ago when she was unhappy. Their father had forced her into a marriage with the Duke of Gostwicke. To add more grief to her misery, her husband had constantly ignored her. Now she sat before him, happier than ever.

"What, no teasing of how I have fallen in love?"

Caroline laughed. "It was only a matter of time before you realized what Lady Eden meant to you. A gentleman does not rant endlessly about a lady unless he holds intense feelings for her. I wanted to knock you in the head over it. However, Gostwicke said I must remain patient for you to discover your feelings on your own. If not, then you wouldn't appreciate the rare gift of love as much."

Falcone stretched out his legs. "Who knew Gostwicke held such clarity on the matters of the heart?"

"Why wouldn't I when I am married to such an amazing lady?" Gostwicke bent to kiss his wife against the lips before sitting down.

His sister gazed adoringly at Gostwicke as if he were the one responsible for the beautiful day. The duke whispered to his sister, inquiring about her health. She blushed at whatever he said, and the duke sat back with a chuckle.

"Did he ever tell you how he pissed off the bloke who shined his face to that color?" Gostwicke quipped.

"No. We haven't touched that subject yet. Victor just finished telling me he has fallen in love," Caroline teased.

"Lady Eden Worthington?" Gostwicke guessed.

Caroline giggled. "Yes."

Falcone groaned. "You two are incorrigible."

Gostwicke laughed. "It took you bloody long enough."

Falcone shook his head at their laughter and smiled at how much lighter he felt by admitting to his love for Eden.

"So who was he?" Gostwicke asked again.

Falcone stared out across the lawn. "Kincaid."

The needles stopped clacking, and his sister reached across to grip Gostwicke's hand out of the corner of his eye. "Why?" she whispered.

Falcone sighed, turning toward them. They needed to discuss this once and for all. Eden was right. He needed to understand what had happened between his sister and Kincaid, so he could relinquish the anger that consumed him whenever he saw Kincaid. He had made a promise to learn the details and he would fulfill his promise now.

"Because I had offended Eden, and Kincaid defended her honor. I was the one at fault," Falcone explained.

"Did your fight have anything to do with what happened in the past?" Caroline whispered.

Falcone shrugged. "I would like to say it didn't, but given the opportunity of throwing punches at one another, I struck back with my revenge for the scandal he embroiled you in."

Caroline sighed. "Oh, Victor. I wish it were as simple as that and I was innocent of any wrongdoing, but that wasn't the case."

"He pursued you, intending to seduce you, knowing all along you were married. You were young and impressionable, not to mention vulnerable," Falcone argued.

Caroline looked at Gostwicke, and he gave her a slight nod to explain what happened with Kincaid. "I may have been young and vulnerable, but I was not an innocent victim. To make Gostwicke jealous, I encouraged Kincaid's pursuit. I didn't understand the pressure he was under, taking over the dukedom after his father passed away shortly before our marriage. In my selfishness, I expected Gostwicke to dote on me, not understanding how he worked night and day."

Caroline paused, gripping the needles. "Since he didn't pay me any attention, I encouraged Kincaid to boast of his success in cuckolding Gostwicke. Even though nothing occurred between myself and Kincaid, I wanted Gostwicke to believe otherwise. I shared a few kisses with the viscount after a ball where I had watched him indulge in drink. Then I whispered my wishes to him and told him where to find Gostwicke. Well, then you know how the rest of it played out."

"How exactly?" Falcone questioned.

"With your sister and I realizing what we almost lost that fateful night," Gostwicke explained. "We spoke with honesty of our feelings and over time have rebuilt our trust in one another. Not every day of a marriage is filled with love and sunshine. Every marriage suffers through moments of darkness, but it is how the couple walks together hand in hand that makes them survive to enjoy those beautiful days of happiness."

"And all is well with your marriage?" Falcone questioned.

Gostwicke settled his hand over Caroline's stomach and shared a smile meant only for the two of them. "Better than it has ever been."

The duke's reaction to Falcone's question proved the love and devotion the couple held for one another. It took him a while to understand the gesture, but it clicked into place once his sister started knitting again. The duke's hand stayed resting on his sister's stomach, and her angelic smile never wavered. Falcone glanced at the pink blanket his sister knitted. They were expecting again and were thrilled.

Falcone had wasted years fuming over an event that hadn't involved him. He had kept his fury alive, proclaiming family honor, when he didn't know the facts of the incident. Eden had been correct all along. While Kincaid was wrong in his actions, he wasn't the only guilty party. If his sister and her husband had found closure with the incident, then so would he. While he couldn't hold a friendship with Kincaid, he would learn to tolerate the gentleman. At least for Eden's sake.

Because he would do anything for her.

Falcone smirked. "So you think this will be a girl?"

"She is hoping so. I hope so too. If not, then the poor lad must endure a nursery filled with everything pink," Gostwicke teased.

Caroline stuck her tongue out at them, which only prompted them to tease her more. The rest of his stay resulted in the same amusement, and he felt a reconnection with his sister, who he had neglected because of his selfish reasons. He promised her he would return soon. Hope blossomed in his heart that, on his return, he would introduce her to Eden.

His wife.

Eden wrapped her arms around her bent legs and rested her head on her knees as she stared out the window in the library. A storm ravaged the garden with its blowing wind and harsh slashes of rain. The dreariness of the day matched her mood perfectly.

She reflected on the past two weeks. They had started with hope and happiness and slowly turned to uncertainty and sorrow.

When Falcone snuck her back inside after another night together, a smile had graced her face for days. She had agreed with enthusiasm when Worth explained what was required of her in helping their mother plan the ball. She had shocked him when she didn't argue for more involvement.

Eden threw herself into the promise she made to Falcone. But with each day slipping into the next and no word from him, she doubted the certainty of their future. Her thoughts soon grew consumed with how she misinterpreted their relationship and how his absence resulted from him seeking his revenge. Then her heart would object, reassuring her what they shared was pure love and that he must have a good reason for not contacting her.

Even the visit she had made to Melody spoke of how honorable of gentleman he was with the best of intentions. She had convinced Worth to take her to see the girl, explaining how Falcone couldn't since he was out of town. It was only right that someone checked on Melody since her beating had resulted from their investigation. He had agreed and stood outside, protecting the house with Kincaid's men while she visited with Agnes and Melody.

During her visit, she had learned how truly gallant Falcone's character actually was. Agnes was the aunt to the girl Falcone blamed himself for killing. When the aunt explained the events surrounding that night, it only proved her theory correct. Agnes had refused to let Falcone support her but had agreed to help him by taking care of the countless victims they encountered through their investigations who were in need of care.

After their discussion, Agnes had gone to the kitchen to prepare lunch for Melody, leaving Eden alone with the girl. It was a miracle the girl recovered. In time, her soul would heal with Agnes's gentle care. Agnes had shared their plans for the future, and it pleased Eden that Agnes would help Melody deal with her nightmares. Melody still struggled, but she had told Eden enough to learn Falcone had never touched the girl once. Melody had clung to her hand while Eden read to her. After a while, the girl had fallen asleep. Eden had stared at her while coming to terms with how cruelly she had treated Falcone all these years. He might project himself to be conceited, but underneath his exterior stood a man more generous and caring than most. Melody and Agnes showed proof of his integrity.

She missed him. More than she thought possible. She missed his smirk and his irritating comments. But most of all, she missed how his arms wrapped around her and held her close to his heart. She missed how his kisses started off slow and gentle, then turned passionate. Eden ached to feel the soft caress of his hands seducing her with the promise of bringing her to the heights of pleasure only he could.

Reese and Graham interrupted her musings when they came into the library. Eden curled deeper into the window seat, hiding behind the curtain. She had pulled it across the seat when she sat down. Eden visited the library to escape with her thoughts.

"Has Falcone been in touch with you since his return?" Reese asked.

When had he returned?

"Yes. We met yesterday morning, and he filled me in on the details of his meeting with Lady Langdale. She was pleased with the invitation he offered. Falcone believes she fell for the bait," Graham explained.

What invitation? Surely not for their ball.

"Is Eden still in the dark regarding the plans for Falcone?" Reese whispered.

What were they keeping from her?

Eden heard footsteps coming closer. "Yes. We already decided that was for the best. Have you changed your mind?"

Yes, Reese, please change your mind.

Reese sighed. "No. I just do not wish to cause Eden any heartache."

Then what secrets are you keeping from me?

"If Eden suffers heartache, then Eden and Falcone were never meant to be," Graham argued.

But they were meant to be. Were they not?

"True. She either trusts him or she does not. Because trust is the most essential element if you love someone. I only hope she can see past his deceit and forgive him in the end," Reese answered.

Love? There was *no doubt that she did.*

"That is why we never shared this part of the plan with her. We need the element of surprise to make this believable," Graham explained.

Whatever they planned, they counted on her reacting with a broken heart.

Reese scoffed. "Surprise? More like a shock. Not only to her but to every guest in attendance."

She could pretend to be in shock.

"Then it will be a success and hopefully an end to Lady L's destruction," Graham said.

Their voices trailed away. Eden's heart floated after listening to their conversation. Falcone hadn't avoided her on purpose because he had changed his mind about them; he acted the part of a callous gentleman who sought his revenge against the Worthingtons by involving himself with the villain. She didn't know the complete details of their plan, but from what she heard, she must play her own part in the drama that was about to unfold.

She only hoped Falcone saw through her act to understand she trusted him and loved him with all her heart. Eden regretted not allowing him to profess his love. She wished he had so that she could've admitted to hers. But like everything else, they would declare their feelings for one another when their hearts demanded.

She missed him something fierce.

Chapter Twenty-Two

AFTER ARRIVING BACK IN town from his sister's estate, Falcone strode into the parlor to find Melody sitting on the sofa with a blanket wrapped around her. She had made a remarkable recovery. Melody smiled shyly at him when he sat down across from her.

"You are looking much better." He spoke softly so as not to scare her. Agnes had told him how loud voices spooked Melody.

Melody nodded. "Yes." Her voice was scratchy.

The physician caring for Melody told him how the beating she endured had damaged her vocal cords. He had stolen so much from her by involving her in this drama.

"I am sorry, Melody, for causing you this trauma. It was never my intention for you to come to any harm," Falcone apologized.

A tear leaked from Melody's eye. "Do not blame yourself too harshly, Lord Falcone. I understood the risks when I involved myself. If I hadn't boasted of my luck, then I would never have suffered from this brutal treatment."

Falcone was unsure how to respond to her confession. "I should have warned you to stay silent."

Melody gripped the blanket. "But you did. Repeatedly. And I ignored your warnings because of my vanity. I wanted to flaunt how special you considered me to the other girls. And with the gentleman callers, I wanted to make them jealous so they would offer me a permanent position as their mistress. You are not to blame."

Falcone attempted a smile but failed. "Ah, but I am. If I never requested your help, you would never have suffered from this beating. And for that, I will continue to hold on to my guilt. I hope you will accept my gratitude by allowing me to provide you with a cottage and a small stipend."

Melody looked down, overwhelmed by his sincerity. "Thank you, my lord."

Falcone stood. "No, thank you, Melody. I wish you a speedy recovery."

Falcone left to find Agnes. He needed to arrange for Melody's departure before Lady Langdale learned Melody had survived and sent men to finish the job. When he returned to town, he didn't care for the rumors circulating around Tabitha's brothel. Lady L had infiltrated the house, taking up headquarters there.

He walked toward the kitchen and found Agnes sitting at the table, enjoying a cup of tea. He sat across from her and waited for her to pour him a cup before broaching the delicate subject.

"She looks well, does she not?" Agnes asked.

"Aye, she does. All because of your tender care," Falcone complimented her.

"When does she leave?"

Falcone took a sip of the warm brew. "As soon as possible."

Agnes nodded. "I thought so. I've seen the extra men guarding the house and realized her time here must end."

"Does she know where she wants to move?"

Agnes offered him a sad smile. "I've told her of my childhood home in Scotland, and she wishes to move there."

Falcone smiled. "That sounds like a refreshing start for Melody."

"And for me too," Agnes stated.

Falcone frowned. "I do not understand."

Agnes placed some biscuits on a plate and slid them over as if he were a child and she needed to explain something difficult to him. "It is time for me to return to my life. Melody has helped me overcome the grief and guilt I clung to since Leslie died. We have agreed upon making the next step in our journey together, and we think Scotland is the perfect setting to do so. Melody is in need of a companion as she continues to heal, and she offers me the sense of family I miss." Agnes gave him a watery smile. "She told me I remind her of her mother."

Falcone reached across the table and placed his hand over hers. "You are both very lucky to have found one another. I wish you both the best of happiness in your days to come. I will make the arrangements."

Agnes rested her other hand on top of his. "And I wish the same for you with Lady Eden. You deserve your own bit of happiness because it is time you free your guilt and love unconditionally."

"I cannot allow myself to forget the trauma I caused." He frowned. "Why do you assume there are feelings between Lady Eden and I?"

"Because we had a pleasant talk when she came to visit Melody."

Falcone's eyebrows drew together in confusion. "Eden came for a visit?"

Agnes nodded. "Yes, and I will tell you what I told her, what I should have told you years ago, but I allowed my own guilty conscience to rule my decisions."

Falcone squeezed her hand. "You have nothing to hold guilt over."

Agnes sighed. "I wish that were so. But I played a much bigger role in that night than you can imagine. May I tell you the truth?"

Falcone pulled his hand away and sat back in his chair. "Please do."

Agnes folded her hands together on top of the table. Her thumbs folded over and over each other in a hypnotic movement. "Leslie suffered terrible pain as her sickness reached its last days. My heart bled for her. I had lived a full life, and she never got the chance to experience the glory of her youth. A gentleman never called on her, danced with her, or stole a kiss from her lips. Leslie dreamed of a knight rescuing her with a secret potion to ease the pain she endured. I overheard my nephew boasting with his friends of a party they were to attend. I knew the lifestyle he led and what type of party it would be."

Agnes stopped to take a sip of tea before she continued. "So I told Leslie she received an invitation to a masquerade ball where she would meet her knight in shining armor." Agnes paused and smiled the most bittersweet smile he had ever seen. "You should have seen her. Leslie leapt out of bed with this newfound energy and pulled on a dress from the wardrobe she had never worn. I pampered her that afternoon with a bath and styled her hair. I can still remember Leslie's sweet smile beaming like a ray of sunshine."

Falcone gulped from the emotions Agnes invoked with her memories. Tears streamed along her cheeks, but she never wiped them away, continuing with the sad tale.

"I arrived with her, pretending to be her lady's maid so I could watch over her. When you approached and flirted with her, I knew by her blush you were her knight."

Falcone scoffed. "My intentions that evening were anything but knightly."

Agnes chuckled. "Oh, I am quite aware, Lord Falcone, of what your intentions were. Rumors circulated of your scandalous carousing, but you were the one who kept the smile beaming on Leslie's face. So I followed you as you led her abovestairs. However, I also noticed Leslie grew weaker. Her energy had slipped away, and the pain that ravaged her body caused her to shake. You probably assumed she trembled because she was nervous." Agnes paused, and Falcone nodded in agreement. "I was the one who slipped the opium in the wine. Her physician urged me to increase the dosage over the past few days. I never imagined an extra dosage would be her demise."

"But I urged her to drink more, so when I took her innocence, it wouldn't frighten her. Because, you see, I sensed she was a virgin and I wanted to claim her for myself."

Agnes gripped his hand again. "No. Stop with your guilt. You were not the cause of her death. She was dying anyway. If not that night, it would have been the next. It is why I gave her a chance to experience all her wishes. Did you hold her in your arms?" Falcone nodded. "Did you kiss her?" Falcone nodded again. "Did you whisper words of her beauty?"

Falcone choked out, "Yes."

"Then you were her savior, Victor. You granted her every wish. She found her knight and drank the special potion that led her on the greatest adventure of her life. You must forgive yourself for this tragedy. Because she has."

Falcone handed Agnes his handkerchief. Her story overwhelmed him, and the words caught in his throat. Agnes had absolved him of the guilt he clung to because he refused to forgive himself. Now she offered him a chance at redemption. But did he deserve it?

"No more guilt, Victor. Allow the chains to drop and forgive yourself. Not only for this but for every action you believe to be your fault. Other people's actions set the course of their destiny. That is no fault of yours," Agnes explained.

Falcone cleared his throat. "I will try."

Agnes wiped her tears away. "That is all I can ask. Now on to something more wonderful."

Falcone smirked. "And what might that be, my dear?"

"When will you marry that glorious lady?"

Falcone laughed at Agnes's description of Eden. Another person who agreed on how glorious she was. "Soon. Very soon."

However, it wasn't soon enough.

Chapter Twenty-Three

E DEN MINGLED WITH THE guests in her family's ballroom as she waited for Falcone to make his dramatic entrance. She had practiced looks of shock and despair in the mirror throughout the afternoon to prepare herself for the unexpected. Every scenario imaginable filtered through her thoughts, but she couldn't imagine one where she would find displeasure with him. However, when she glanced at the entryway, she hadn't prepared herself for who walked beside him, clinging to his arm.

Lady Ravencroft strutted next to him like she belonged at the ball. The ball was in honor of her sons' marriages to Maggie and Noel. It should've guaranteed her an invitation. But they had left her name off the guest list for a reason. Both gentlemen had broken off ties with their mother and refused to share their lives with her. Why did Falcone escort the lady to the ball?

For his revenge. What else? She noticed his smirk as he led Lady Ravencroft deeper into the ballroom. Whispers surrounded her. When he walked them over to her, a sharp pain overtook her chest, as if someone had slit her heart open.

"Lady Ravencroft, allow me to introduce you to Lady Eden. She is the *older* sister of your daughters-in-law." Falcone smirked, his eyes lit with his arrogance.

"I have heard of her but never imagined she held such beauty. You have excellent taste, my lord." Lady Ravencroft's voice dropped to a whisper. "I hope you hold no bitterness toward Falcone for enjoying his bit of fun with you. You must understand how he requires a lady with more experience in meeting his needs. If it doesn't bother you, then I do not mind sharing. The more, the merrier, I always say."

"You are more than welcome to have him for yourself," Eden snarled.

Lady Ravencroft ran her hand along Falcone's lapel. "I had hoped you would say so."

Eden fought the tears back as heartache tore through her soul. She bit her tongue to keep from sobbing. Practice never helped to prepare you for the reality of having one's heart broken.

Lady Ravencroft turned her attention toward her sons and strode off toward them. Eden expected Falcone to follow her. Instead, he lifted her hand to his lips and kissed her knuckles.

"Your snarl does not disappoint, my glorious vixen, but gives me the courage to continue," Falcone whispered before following Lady Ravencroft.

Eden pressed her knuckles against her cheek to soak in his warmth. A slight whimper escaped as his words sank in. Then she remembered what Reese and Graham had expressed. If she didn't believe in him, then she had never trusted Falcone to begin with, therefore never loving him at all. Her eyes trailed after him, watching his every move. He never once held onto Lady Ravencroft. It was the lady who clung to him. The smile gracing his face was false. It wasn't one he shared with her when he found her amusing. He played a part that she wasn't privy to, but she would pretend to show everyone how distraught she was for his disregard.

Soon, Eden found herself surrounded by her sisters. Maggie and Noel stayed close to her side as they watched Lady Ravencroft work the room with Falcone following behind her, making introductions when needed.

"We want to apologize, Eden, for not warning you, but Graham said it was vital for you to act surprised," Noel whispered.

Eden turned an astonished gaze on her sisters. "You both knew?" They nodded, and Eden swallowed back a sob. "Of course. I understand."

Maggie wrapped an arm around her waist. "Do you? Because I fear any second now you are on the verge of breaking down."

Eden shook her head, biting her bottom lip. "I am fine. What else has everyone kept from me?"

Maggie and Noel exchanged a glance. Then Maggie said, "All the ladies are to welcome Lady Ravencroft into their fold with invitations to tea or an event they plan to host."

It all became clear to her now. They were drawing Lady Ravencroft into their web of acceptance so she would switch her loyalty to them. It was quite brilliant. They wanted to convince Lady Ravencroft of the power she held by Eden acting like a lady spurned. But to continue with her act, she couldn't tell her sisters of her plan. It was time to switch the element of surprise onto her family, friends, and Lord Falcone himself.

She pasted on a smile. "I hope the plan is a success, then. If you will excuse me, I promised Mama I would help direct the servants when to serve the cake."

Before they could stop her, she moved on. However, she didn't get very far before Graham stopped her with Lord Nolting in tow.

"There you are, Eden. We have looked for you everywhere."

Eden raised a questioning brow at her brother. "May I inquire as to why?"

She stared at them, waiting for an explanation. When none came forth, Graham nudged Lord Nolting with his elbow.

Lord Nolting winced. "I wish to ask you if you would do me the honor of accompanying me on the next dance."

Eden pinched her lips. "I thought you did not wish to associate yourself with me."

"Well . . . That is, I . . ." Nolting stuttered.

Graham stepped in to explain. "Nolting is attempting to say how I explained the unfortunate incident with Falcone. He now understands how the marquess stepped out of line."

"Yes. Also, your mother told me how upset you were and I told myself I would give you another chance," Nolting boasted.

"Another chance?" Eden snarled.

Nolting nodded. "It is the least I can do after abandoning you as I did."

Eden glared at Graham, shaking her head at his interference, before transferring her glare to Lord Nolting. "Let me see if I understand this. You are offering me another chance to be seen on your arm out of the goodness of your heart. And this is only because my *mother* and *brother* clarified the situation for you. When my word that day in the park held no appeal to you whatsoever." She paused. "Well, Lord Nolting, you may take your dance and sh—"

"Eden, I must talk with you. I need to explain . . ." Falcone grabbed Eden's arm and swung her around. He dropped her arm when he saw her furious expression.

Eden wondered if this evening would ever end. Or if it would continue to torment her with one incident after another. She turned to Nolting. "A dance you say?"

When he nodded, she grabbed his hand and marched them to the dance floor.

Eden didn't remember a single aspect of the dance she shared with Lord Nolting. She had focused her attention on Falcone and Graham. They appeared caught up in an argument. Over what, she held no clue. And at this point, she no longer cared. She wanted to escape to her bedchamber, close her eyes, and disappear for the evening.

Lord Nolting rattled on about how important it was for him to keep the company of a virtuous lady. Well, she hated to disappoint the earl, but he ruined his chances by dancing with her. Eden would find humor at the irony if her emotions weren't so strung out. While she understood Falcone acted a part, his betrayal by staying silent stung. Nor did she much care for another lady touching him.

Lord Nolting escorted her back to Graham after they finished their dance. Falcone remained by his side with his arms folded across his chest. He scowled at Lord Nolting.

"I thought I told you to stay away from this bloke," Falcone snarled.

Eden smirked. "And I chose to ignore you."

Falcone snapped his fingers in the air. "Tell your puppy to scamper away."

Nolting puffed out his chest. "Now see here, Lord Falcone. I am under the impression your attention is unwanted by the lady."

Falcone took a threatening step toward Nolting. "Someone has misinformed you. Now you can either leave on your own or I shall help you along."

Nolting gasped. "Well, I never." He turned to Eden. "Lady Eden, your family has fed me false information about you. I can no longer associate myself with a lady of your character."

Falcone grasped Nolting by his lapels. "Lady Eden possesses an impeccable character. You are lucky she even graced you with a minute of her time. If you so much as slander her again, I will make you regret it. Do I make myself clear, Lord Nolting?"

Nolting nodded repeatedly. Falcone dropped him, and the earl scampered away like Falcone had demanded.

Eden stomped her foot at the scene he caused. "You are an unbelievable, boorish oaf who once again caused a scene with your jealous rant. You have some nerve after strutting around all evening with another lady on your arm."

"I can explain," Falcone pleaded.

She held up a hand. "I do not wish to hear a single word of your deception."

Graham stepped in between their argument and guided them toward the terrace, away from the curious gazes of their peers. "Perhaps you two need a little privacy for this conversation."

"There is nothing I wish to discuss with Lord Falcone," Eden hissed.

"Eden, please hear him out." Graham glanced across the terrace, something stealing his attention away from them. "If you give him a chance . . ." His gaze narrowed as he stared at the young lady talking with Colebourne. "Who is she? Do either of you recognize the guest Colebourne is talking with?"

Eden rolled her eyes. Just like a lady in a pretty skirt to distract her brother from their conversation. She glanced at the lady but didn't know who she was. "No. Nor do I care. Perhaps Lord Falcone is familiar with the lady. With his past carousing, he probably knows her quite well."

"Eden, you misunderstand," Falcone stated.

"I do not believe I do," she snarled.

"Do you know who the girl is, Falcone?" Graham interrupted.

Falcone growled, taking a swift glance at the girl. "She looks familiar, but I cannot place her."

"I stand correct," Eden gloated.

"Excuse me," Graham muttered, and he hurried toward Colebourne.

Falcone grabbed Eden by the arms, holding her still so she wouldn't disappear on him. He only had a few minutes alone with her before Lady Ravencroft found him. And he couldn't afford Lady Ravencroft catching him apologizing to Eden.

"Unhand me, Falcone."

"Victor."

"Falcone."

"It is in your best interest to follow the lady's command," Lady Chesterton said from behind them. "Your companion for the evening is on her way over to you. While the lady's glare will help the situation, your pleading will not."

Falcone glanced over his shoulder, then through the terrace doors to see that Lady Ravencroft walked toward them. He dropped his hands from Eden's arms while Lady Chesterton stepped between them.

She slipped her hands inside his suit coat, pretending to show him affection while she stood on her tiptoes and whispered a warning in his ear. "Lady L has arrived. The show will begin soon."

Eden's fury rose to another level as she witnessed the intimate exchange between Falcone and Lady Chesterton. Lady Ravencroft strolled toward them on Lord Chesterton's arm, returning from their dance. Her gloating expression made Eden uneasy.

"You are the sly gentleman I thought you were. Are you making plans for a ménage later this evening? Or have you already shared in the pleasures of the flesh with one another?" She shook her head as she glanced between the two ladies. "No, I do not believe your two lovers have shared you together."

Lady Chesterton attempted to change the subject. "How nice to see you again, Lady Ravencroft. Did you enjoy your dance with my husband?"

"Ah, yes. He is quite a skillful dancer, which only leads me to believe he would perform very well in bed. But I wonder if he is as skillful as you, Lady Chesterton." Lady Ravencroft turned toward Eden. "I only say this because the last time I saw Lady Chesterton, she had her head nestled in Lord Falcone's lap while he offered for me to join them. I, however, declined and explored the brothel for my own pleasures. When I returned to their room, they were both naked in bed and Lady Chesterton rode Lord Falcone's cock, screaming his name. The marquess let out quite a roar at the pleasure she gave him. It was quite exhilarating to watch."

Eden gasped, and Falcone watched her rosy cheeks pale as if she saw a ghost. She rushed away, stumbling against the other guests to get away from them.

"Eden," Falcone shouted and started after her.

But Lady Ravencroft gripped his sleeve, holding him back. "Let her go, my dear. She will forgive you in time. It's not like she has any other options."

Falcone shook off her hold. "What do you mean by that?"

Lady Ravencroft flipped her hair over her shoulder. "Why, she is practically on the shelf. A lady of her age has very limited choices. She would be foolish to walk away from someone of your standing. Especially when you can have any young miss you so choose. Believe me, the girl is too wise to be so ungrateful."

Falcone fumed over the delay Lady Ravencroft cost him. However, she refused to let him go.

"Now, I need you to make a few more introductions," she demanded and looked at the Chestertons. "Thank you for the dance, my lord. Until we meet again."

She led Falcone away, right into a trap he should've been expecting. But the pain expressed in Eden's eyes before she ran away occupied his every thought. Lady Ravencroft didn't lead him to other guests for him to make introductions to. However, she led him to one guest he knew for a fact wasn't on the guest list. Barbara Langdale. Lady Chesterton had warned him, but the warning had come too late. Falcone only hoped she warned the others in time.

Falcone followed Lady Ravencroft down the balcony stairs and into the garden. It wasn't until they were deep within that someone lit a lantern. Lady L emerged out of the shadows like an apparition.

"Lord Falcone, how kind of you to invite us to this amazing ball. I must admit, I never thought you would actually betray the Worthingtons like you have." Lady L circled around him as she talked.

"As I explained before, I wish to seek my revenge against them and the Duke of Colebourne," Falcone said.

"Ahh, yes. The duke must fall, too. And what better opportunity for their fall from grace than this evening? I have everything in place."

Falcone rubbed his hands together. "Excellent."

Lady L stopped before him. "Except for one detail. I have decided you shall be perfect for the job."

Uneasiness settled over Falcone. "And that is?"

Lady L snapped her fingers, and her two guards came to her side. "You will escort my men inside and draw everyone's attention at the ball. Then you will inform them they can either discard their jewels and money or they will perish."

"Perish? You never mentioned your revenge resulted in the death of innocent lives," Falcone argued.

Lady L laughed. "First, none of those people are innocent. Every single one of them performs a sin every day. Whether it be immoral or honorable makes no difference. And 'tis only a threat."

"When I offered my services, it was in secrecy so I do not ruin my upstanding name. If I make this threat, they will accuse me of treason."

Lady L shrugged. "Then I guess you shouldn't have gotten into bed with the devil." She pointed at the Worthingtons' townhome. "Now move or my guards will make sure you do."

Falcone stalled. How could he escape from the guards and warn the others? Lady Ravencroft latched onto him to walk them out of the garden, with the guards flanking their sides.

"Oh, I forgot to mention how Lady Ravencroft will stay by your side to make sure you follow my orders. Do show him how you plan to keep him close by, Lady Ravencroft." Lady L's taunts echoed behind them.

Once they reached the balcony stairs, he felt the barrel of a small pistol digging into his side. They reached the terrace faster than he had hoped. When they walked into the ballroom, the crowd separated. They stared at the men towering over them, strolling through the ballroom as if they were guests, too.

Lady Ravencroft steered them toward the musicians. "I thank you for allowing me to shine for one night, Lord Falcone. It was a delightful touch you and your friends added by having so many ladies invite me to call on them." She made a tsking noise. "However, when will any of you learn you cannot outsmart Lady Langdale? She is brilliant and predicts every move made against her."

Falcone didn't understand, but Lady Ravencroft waited for the dance to end before starting the terror Lady L had planned. Falcone searched the room for Eden, but he couldn't find her anywhere. However, he saw Kincaid, who gave him a suspicious stare. He nodded his head at Lady Ravencroft and swiped at his face, pointing his finger like a gun. Kincaid nodded that he understood the hint. He whispered something to his wife, and Jacqueline took off toward her family. Kincaid moved throughout the crowd, stopping to deliver a message to the many guards they had in disguise.

Once the dance ended, Lady Ravencroft spoke to the musicians to play a short piece to draw everyone's attention. While they waited, she motioned for the servant carrying a tray of glasses filled with champagne over to them. She passed a glass to Falcone and then grabbed one for herself, all the while keeping the pistol aimed at him. "Ladies and gentlemen, may I have your attention?" she shouted to the crowd. "I wish to congratulate my sons on making such profitable matches. You have done well, Crispin and Gregory."

A hush fell over the crowd for a brief second before whispers circulated. It was only knowledge to the Worthington family and close friends that Dracott and Ravencroft were brothers. Lady L had started the next phase in her game of revenge by exposing the Worthingtons' secret.

"If you will, please keep your attention focused our way for a second longer. Lord Falcone has a request he would like to make." Lady Ravencroft lifted her glass in a silent toast to herself. After she drained the glass, she tilted her head for him to move forward.

He refused to persecute himself for this cause. He had risked more than he wanted to bring Lady L to justice. Because of the risks he took, he had lost the most important person who mattered.

However, he stepped forward, if for no other reason than to stall until he received the signal that everyone stood ready to fight.

A battle to conquer blindfolded.

Chapter Twenty-Four

E DEN RAN ALONG THE hallway, getting as far away from Falcone and the depraved souls surrounding him. She thought she could pretend his deceit never affected her, but in truth, it left her an emotional mess. She pressed against the wall, catching her breath. When she heard the whispered voices coming from around the corner, she stepped deeper into the shadows. She couldn't bear to speak to anyone right now.

"We must hurry. They have already revealed the first signal."

"I am, but this bag is heavy."

One voice cackled. "The heavier, the better. More blunt we will receive from Lady L."

Eden gasped. The voices were from Lady L's crew, and they were robbing her home. They rounded the corner, carrying two bags. They had snuck into the coatroom and stole the furs the guests had worn to the ball.

"When were they to light the fire?"

Eden frowned. They weren't attempting arson, were they?

"After the second signal. They mean to trap the toffs inside the ballroom unless they part with their precious jewels. Lady L is forcing Falcone to make the demand for them to hand over their riches. It is her revenge for him double-crossing her.

Then she plans to kill him, but not before everyone whispers his name as the one who caused the tragedy."

Their voices drifted away, and Eden took off in the opposite direction. She had to warn Falcone of what Lady L planned. She only hoped she wasn't too late. Oh, why had she run away from him? Why hadn't she fought for him? Deceit be damned.

Eden tore into the ballroom, straight into Graham.

"Eden, you must leave. Kincaid has the carriages ready to take you to safety. Mama and the girls are waiting for you." Graham grabbed her arm and ushered her toward the foyer.

Eden broke loose. "No, I must find Falcone. There is a plot asunder that will ruin his name. We must warn him."

"It is too late for that. Please, listen to me and leave now," Graham pleaded.

Eden swiveled around as she searched for Falcone. She saw him near the musicians with Lady Ravencroft, waiting for the dance to end. She clutched at Graham's sleeve. "They are planning a fire."

"Where?" Graham demanded.

"Near the ballroom, to give the guests an illusion of how they will burn if they do not follow their directions," Eden explained.

Graham and Eden turned in circles, searching for the danger she had overheard.

"There." Eden pointed toward two burly men leaving a room they kept for the servants to exchange trays during the ball. It led to a set of stairs below where the servants worked to prepare the savory desserts everyone enjoyed eating at the ball.

Graham rushed toward the room, but he was already too late. Smoke was leaking from the opening near the top of the door. Eden ran after him to help, tearing off her gloves and covering her nose and mouth as she ventured deeper into the smoke. Graham had ripped off his coat, slapping at the flames until he put them out. They had arrived in time to stop this part of the threat.

Graham kicked the door leading downstairs open and started down the steps. He soon emerged with a lady clutched to his side. "Help her while I get the servants to safety."

Eden stepped forward in the haze of smoke to grab the lady. She noticed it was Lady Chesterton and she was clutching her side. Blood soaked her fingers and gown. Eden wrapped her arm around Lady Chesterton and led her outside. They collapsed on the terrace floor, coughing from the smoke they had inhaled.

She clutched at Eden's hand. "Forgive"—she gasped for breath—"him."

"Shh. Save your strength," Eden urged.

"Too late." Lady Chesterton coughed. "Tried to warn them. I was too late."

"No, you weren't. You saved them."

Lady Chesterton's body shook in Eden's grasp. Her mumbling grew worse, along with her coughing. Eden ripped off the ribbon tied around her waist and pressed it against the bleeding. Someone had stabbed Lady Chesterton in her attempt to save the servants.

"Lady Eden," Lady Chesterton whispered.

"Yes."

"Nothing happened that night. We pretended so we could save Melody." She gasped for a breath. "Please forgive him."

Tears poured along Eden's cheeks. Eden had misjudged this lady, too. Lady Chesterton lay dying on her lap, and instead of worrying about herself, she pleaded with Eden to forgive Falcone for another gallant act.

"I will," Eden choked out. "I do."

Lady Chesterton smiled at Eden before drawing her last breath. Eden cried for the injustice that had brought this lady to her demise. When would this terror ever end?

Screams pierced the air when darkness suffocated the ballroom. Soon, chaos descended on the terrace. Guests ran outside toward the stairs, while Lady L's crew struck with their act of terror. Some ran after the guests, while others fought the men Kincaid had assigned to guard the party. Eden shook with fright. With Lady Chesterton lying on her skirts, preventing her from rising, she had trapped herself. The best she could do was pull them back between the decorative pots.

Eden watched as two guards led Falcone outside by his arms. Lady Ravencroft tittered on her heels behind them, ranting about how Falcone would meet his demise for defying Lady L's orders. Soon, Ralston and Kincaid appeared and bashed the two guards on the head with wooden clubs. This caused the guards to stumble around, knocking into Lady Ravencroft and sending her falling to the ground.

Falcone jerked around and helped Ralston and Kincaid secure the guards against the posts. After they tied up the guards, Falcone held his hand out to Kincaid in an offer of gratitude. Kincaid returned the handshake.

"Falcone," Eden whispered. "Victor."

He raised his head, searching the terrace. Falcone heard Eden, but he couldn't find her anywhere. His heart raced. He thought Graham had gotten her to safety.

"Eden!" he shouted, looking into the darkness. "Where are you?"

Lady Ravencroft cackled. "It does not matter where she is, Lord Falcone. Because you are about to meet your demise."

Falcone's eyes finally adjusted to the darkness, and he saw Eden sitting near the plants with someone lying across her lap. However, Lady Ravencroft stood in front of the woman he loved and pointed her gun back and forth between them. She aimed it at him and pulled back the trigger.

"Victor!" Eden's shout ripped through the air, piercing his heart and shattering it in two.

The bullet ripped through him, and he fell to his knees. He stretched his hands out before him to break his fall before collapsing. In a blur, he watched Kincaid and Ralston tackle Lady Ravencroft and rip the gun away from her hands. Eden's chants of "No, no, no!" echoed all around him before he slipped unconscious.

Eden tried to shove Lady Chesterton off her. Her cries filled the air as she struggled to get to Victor. Someone soon came to her aid and moved Lady Chesterton away. She crawled over to Victor and gathered him in her arms, her tears soaking his bloodstained clothes.

"Somebody please help him." Eden pleaded. Her fingers trembled as they trailed over him. "I love you, Victor. Do you hear me? Do not die on me. I need you."

Eden clung to his hand, crying more desperately as she felt his warmth disappearing into a chill of despair.

She fought those who stole him away and those who offered her comfort. It wasn't until Reese carried her in his arms to her bedchamber did her hysterics calm. He offered his support as he had done when they were children and their father bullied her. He had always been her protector, and she loved him for it. But it wasn't his arms she wished to protect her anymore.

"I waited too long," Eden murmured.

Reese held her hand while she lay curled on her side. "For what?"

"To tell him I loved him," Eden whispered. "I wouldn't even let him tell me how he felt."

"It is never too late to tell anyone how much you love them."

Eden didn't respond. She couldn't without breaking down again. They had yet to tell them if he survived. The surgeon was with him now in a bedchamber down the hall.

Reese squeezed her hand. "He loved you, and he knew you loved him, too. A man wouldn't make the sacrifices he did if it were not for love."

"What happens if he does not make it?" Eden choked out.

Reese winked at her. "What happens if he does? Will you put the bloke out of his misery?"

Eden attempted a laugh. "Still trying to marry me off, are you?"

Reese smiled. "I must, my dear sister. For once you are married, Mother has given me permission to torment Graham into finding a bride."

Eden smiled for the first time that evening. "Then I will make the ultimate sacrifice, but only on one condition."

Reese arched his eyebrow. "And what might that be?"

"You allow me to partake in the torment."

Reese chuckled. "Agreed."

A light knock sounded on the door before Graham poked his head inside. His serious expression didn't bode well for the news he was about to deliver.

Eden sat up, gripping Reese's hand. "Falcone?"

Graham took a deep breath. "He lives."

Eden raised her other hand to her mouth, fighting back more tears. "Oh, that is the most wonderful news."

"What are you not telling us?" Reese demanded.

Graham rubbed his eyes. "Nothing severe. Falcone must remain in bed for a week to make a full recovery. He was lucky, and the bullet made a clean exit right below his shoulder."

"Then why the morbid expression?" Reese asked.

Graham dropped into a chair. "Because the events of the evening finally hit me full force. I cannot believe the amount of destruction caused. Lady Chesterton died, Lady Ravencroft shot Falcone, and our sister had to witness the brutality of it all. And still Lady Langdale escaped capture. It is a bit overwhelming."

Reese rose and gripped Graham's shoulder. "Yes, it is. However, look at what we accomplished this evening. We now have Lady Ravencroft and the majority of Lady L's crew behind bars. Her organization has diminished to a minuscule number from when she started this evening. Lady Chesterton's death is unfortunate, but think of the lives we saved with your quick thinking. Falcone has survived, and your sister is stronger than you give her credit for."

"We are sorry, Eden. Can you ever forgive us for keeping our plans silent?" Graham asked.

Eden slid off the bed and grabbed each of her brothers' hands. "Yes. Now scoot, I must change."

Graham frowned. "Whatever for?"

Reese laughed, pulling his brother out of the chair. "I think our sister wants to sneak into a certain guest's bedchamber for a scandalous interlude."

Graham dug his heels in. "And you are permitting her to do so?" Graham asked in shock.

Reese winked at Eden. "She has something she wishes to tell Falcone, and it cannot wait a second longer."

Eden laughed as Reese dragged Graham from her bedchamber. After they left, she twirled around in a circle at the joy she felt at Victor surviving. She made swift work of undressing and cleaning the blood off before pulling on a nightgown and robe. She snuck along the hallway to the guest wing. Since only one room had a closed door, it must be where they had placed Victor. She eased the door open and slipped inside. The fire glowed, casting light across the room.

She walked closer to the bed, where Victor was lying against the bedsheets, fast asleep.

She choked back a sob at how he miraculously looked alive. His shoulder wrapped in bandages was the only indication of his injury. Eden laid her robe across the chair and crawled onto the bed. She laid her head on the pillow and slid her fingers into the hand curled at his side.

"I love you," she whispered before closing her eyes to fall asleep next to him.

Chapter Twenty-Five

FALCONE FORCED HIS EYELIDS open, only to close them again when he saw spots and a wave of dizziness overcame him. Burning pain tore into his shoulder. He lifted his arm to ease the ache and almost screamed when the agony overtook him.

He managed to open his eyes to see he lay in an unfamiliar room. When he went to rub his eyes, a heavy weight on his hand prevented him from doing so. He looked down to see fingers entwined with his. As his gaze rose higher, he saw Eden lying next to him, clinging to his hand as if she feared she had lost him.

Then the nightmare flooded back to him. The horror of the evening played out in slow motion. His fear of Lady Ravencroft pointing the gun in Eden's direction was the most frightening experience of his life. The life he had planned for them had flashed before him. When Lady Ravencroft pulled the trigger in his direction, Falcone had only felt relief that Lady Ravencroft spared Eden's life. Her cries still echoed in his ears.

"I love you," Falcone whispered before pain dragged him back under.

The next time Falcone awoke, it was to find Eden staring at him, still clinging to his hand. Tears streamed along her cheeks.

"Ahh, love." He groaned. "Why are you crying?"

"Because I almost lost you."

He attempted to chuckle but winced at the pain. "It will take more than a bullet for you to lose me."

Eden lifted their hands to her lips and kissed his palm. "Do you promise?"

"Yes. Now come closer," Falcone ordered.

"But your wound?"

"Is on the other side of my body. This side is perfectly healthy and aches for your touch," Falcone argued.

Eden slid closer, and Falcone wrapped his good arm around her, squeezing softly. "Ahh, I have missed you so much. The past two weeks have been unbearable without you snarling at me."

Eden slapped his chest. "Well, 'tis your own fault for keeping your smirk away and not being honest with me."

Falcone sighed. "I regret what we did. It wasn't fair to you for what we put you through."

"While it hurt when I discovered the truth, I understood the reasons behind your deceit."

"I deceived you and all for what? To capture some lady who is so elusive, it is impossible." Falcone scoffed.

Eden rolled over, being gentle so as not to disturb his wound. She caressed his face, easing away his stress. "Enough about Lady Langdale. There is something I wish to declare."

Falcone pressed his finger against her lips. "I can wait until you are ready. Do not utter them now out of fear of losing me. Declare them when your heart is ready."

"*Falcone*," Eden snarled at his interruption.

Falcone smirked. "*Lady Eden*." He chuckled at her expression. It was one of confliction. He loved when he ruffled her emotions. "Eden?"

Her reply was to press her lips against his in a soft kiss that warmed the heart, with soft slow strokes of their tongues, meeting and pulling away to intertwine.

"Victor."

He stared at her with his eyes heavy with desire. "Mmm."

"I love you with all my heart. You are the other half of my soul that I have kept at arm's length all these years because of the emotions you brought to the surface that frightened me. Emotions I wish to share with you every day for the rest of our lives."

"Ahh, love. I never realized it then, but I believe you stole my heart the very first time we met and you called me out for my rakish ways. I love you, Eden Worthington, to the depths of my soul," Falcone declared.

Eden gazed adoringly into Victor's eyes, just the way he had imagined she would when they admitted to their feelings. It was a look he would spend a lifetime cherishing for her to bestow on him.

"Just so you know, my brother is aware I snuck into your bedchamber. So he might force you to take me for your bride. You understand how servants talk. There is sure to be a scandal over my visit," Eden warned with a smile.

"Then perhaps we should make sure a scandal occurs. I wouldn't want the whispers to be false," Victor suggested.

A wicked smile lifted Eden's lips. She sat up and slipped the nightgown over her head, bringing forth a groan from Victor.

"An excellent idea, Falcone." Eden swept the blanket off him as her gaze raked his form. "An excellent idea indeed."

"Victor," he growled.

And his demand was granted as they brought each other pleasure with their lovemaking.

Victor didn't know what he ever did to deserve the love of a glorious vixen. He only knew that he would never take life for granted again. Each day he would spend thanking his lucky stars for being able to love Eden. The gift of her love was a welcoming balm for his past mistakes and the guilt that plagued him. With her love, his soul found redemption.

Eden cried as she lay wrapped in Victor's warm embrace. They were tears of happiness. Victor's love washed away her fears, her loneliness, the bitterness she clung to so she would never get hurt. He gifted her with the security she had always longed for. He wiped away her tears and murmured how much he cherished her. She rejoiced at the love overflowing from her heart. With his love, she was able to free herself from every fear imaginable.

Because love held the magical touch of making anything possible.

Epilogue

F ALCONE WRAPPED HIS ARMS around Eden, bringing her against his chest as they watched the carriage travel down the road from his townhome. He blanched at the slight twinge, but once her soft curves nestled against him, his ache eased. It had been a month since Lady Ravencroft shot him, and the wound took longer to heal than he wished for.

The goodbyes Agnes and Melody spoke were bittersweet for him. It was a part of his past he must lay to rest so he could enjoy a future with Eden.

"They will be well," Eden reassured them. "Plus, Agnes promised to write weekly."

Falcone smiled at Eden's positive outlook on Agnes's and Melody's journey. "I may worry if I so choose, Lady Falcone."

Eden turned in his arms, smiling at him. "I know, 'tis one of the many reasons I love you so."

Falcone brushed his lips across hers. He never could resist stealing a kiss. "And the other many reasons are?"

Eden stood on her tiptoes and whispered in his ear, "The list is too long. It might be more sensible for us to retire to our bedchamber to discuss it at length. Also, I noticed how your shoulder is giving you trouble. I suggest bed rest for the remainder of the day."

Falcone lifted Eden in his arms to show her how perfectly fit he was and strode inside their home. By now, the servants were quite used to the displays of affection and would vanish once they saw them expressing it so. "Perhaps it is you who requires the bed rest. I would be more than happy to listen to your reasons. That way, I can share mine with you while you rest."

Eden wrapped her arms around Falcone's neck. "And why would I need bed rest, Lord Falcone?"

Falcone laid Eden on their bed and brushed the hair back from her face. "Because, Lady Falcone, I hear it is very important for a lady in your condition to rest."

An impish smile spread across Eden's face at their playfulness. It was a far cry from their snarls and smirks. Not that they still didn't share those with one another. After all, it was what had sparked their attraction.

"Are you pleased?" Eden asked.

Falcone pressed a kiss against Eden's stomach. "More than you can imagine, my love."

"I love you, Victor."

"And I love you, my fiery vixen."

He spent the day worshiping Eden as she deserved. The troubles that awaited them could wait another day. For now, they were two souls who lost themselves in each other and the love that surrounded them.

A love only meant for them.

Read Graham's story in
The Siren's Gentleman

"Thank you for reading The Fiery Vixen. Gaining exposure as an independent author relies mostly on word-of-mouth, so if you have the time and inclination, please consider leaving a short review wherever you can."

Want to join my mailing list? Visit https://www.lauraabarnes.com/contact-newsletter today!

Desire other books to read by Laura A. Barnes

Enjoy these other historical romances:

Fate of the Worthingtons Series
The Tempting Minx
The Seductive Temptress
The Fiery Vixen
The Siren's Gentleman

Matchmaking Madness Series
How the Lady Charmed the Marquess
How the Earl Fell for His Countess
How the Rake Tempted the Lady
How the Scot Stole the Bride
How the Lady Seduced the Viscount
How the Lord Married His Lady

Tricking the Scoundrels Series:
Whom Shall I Kiss... An Earl, A Marquess, or A Duke?
Whom Shall I Marry... An Earl or A Duke?
I Shall Love the Earl
The Scoundrel's Wager
The Forgiven Scoundrel

Romancing the Spies Series:
Rescued By the Captain
Rescued By the Spy
Rescued By the Scot

About Author Laura A. Barnes

International selling author Laura A. Barnes fell in love with writing in the second grade. After her first creative writing assignment, she knew what she wanted to become. Many years went by with Laura filling her head full of story ideas and some funny fish songs she wrote while fishing with her family. Thirty-seven years later, she made her dreams a reality. With her debut novel *Rescued By the Captain*, she has set out on the path she always dreamed about.

When not writing, Laura can be found devouring her favorite romance books. Laura is married to her own Prince Charming (who for some reason or another thinks the heroes in her books are about him) and they have three wonderful children and two sweet grandbabies. Besides her love of reading and writing, Laura loves to travel. With her passport stamped in England, Scotland, and Ireland; she hopes to add more countries to her list soon.

While Laura isn't very good on the social media front, she loves to hear from her readers. You can find her on the following platforms:

You can visit her at ***www.lauraabarnes.com*** to join her mailing list.

Website: https://www.lauraabarnes.com/

Amazon: https://amazon.com/author/lauraabarnes

Goodreads: https://www.goodreads.com/author/show/16332844.Laura_A_Barnes

Facebook: https://www.facebook.com/AuthorLauraA.Barnes/

Instagram: https://www.instagram.com/labarnesauthor/

Twitter: https://twitter.com/labarnesauthor

BookBub: https://www.bookbub.com/profile/laura-a-barnes

TikTok: https://www.tiktok.com/@labarnesauthor

Manufactured by Amazon.ca
Bolton, ON

31309545R00139